Bad Luck

CURSED MANUSCRIPTS
BOOK 5

IAIN ROB WRIGHT

ULCERATED PRESS

With thanks to my awesome patreons.
Michael Pearse, Mark Ayre, Virginia Milway, Suzie Roush, Katrice Tuck, Adrian Shotbolt, Minnis Hendricks, Kelli Herrera, Terrie-Ann Thulborn, Phil Brady, Steve Haessler, Jackie Grocutt, Darrion Mika, Karen Lewis, Suzy Tadlock, Kaarin Chadwick, Mari Meisel, Jayne Smith, Susanne Stohr, CJMac, Stacey, Amanda Shaw, Connie France, Gillian Moon, Robin, Armando Llerena, Stephanie Everett, Linda Heafield, Ali Black, Elizabeth Thompson, Stainedglasslee, Stacey Guitarmangrg, Angela Richards, Diane Rushton, Stephen Moss, Jean Geill, Elizabeth Auclair, Adrianne Yang, Joy Perry, Linda, Leslie Clutton, Sarah Chambers, Sylvia Camposano, Kat Miller, Susan Crouch, Sara Boe, Carole, Nigel Crabtree, Becky Wright, Claire Taylor, Caryn Larsen, Leigh Hickey, Jenny Ibbs, Steve Griffith, Diesta Kaiser, Fiona Thompson, Cherise Fugue, Mark Horey, Gian Spadone, Mark Stone, Rachel LaFraniere, Deborah Shelton, Pauline Stout, Angelica Maria, Katie Potter, Jordan Rasmussen, Deirdre Lydon, Bobbie Kelley, Vicky Salter, Melissa Potter, Debbi Sansom, 44bats, Nicole Reid, Bruce W Clark, Carrieanne, Chris Viehman, Mark Harvey, Kristina Goeke, Mark Simpson, Graeme McMechan, Jacqueline Coleman, Vanda Luty, Ruth F Phelps, Donna Twells, Katie Warburton, Susan Kay, Nick Brooks, Stewart Barnes, Nigel Jopson, Gemma Ve, Steven Barnett, Andrew Moss, Sally Jayne Dainton, Tania Buss, Steve Irvine, Lee Ballard, Clive The Moose, Xya Marie, Robert Smith, Oscar Booker Jr, Trevor Oakley, Leona Overton, Susan Hayden, Jennifer Holston, Kelee S, Terence Smith, Michelle Chaney, Roy Oswald, Paul

Weaver, Linda Robinson, Chris Aitchison, Michael Rider, Deborah Knapp Bread, Beth Thurman, Cass Griffiths, Debbie Ivory, David Lennox, Zoe Lloyd, William Matthews, Hazel Smith, Gary Harper, Laurie Cook, Margaret McAloon, Paul, Neil Grey, Catherine H, Sherrie, Brian McGowan, Pam Felten, Carol Wicklund, Mary Meisel, Deborah, Lady Aliehs, Rachel Mayfield, Erica Lewis, Mary Stephenson, Maniel Le, Tara Enright, Andre Jenkin, Lawrence Clamons, Gary Groves, Mike Prankard, Dorothy Rushforth, Dan Garay, Lynn Mcvay, Rona Trout, Mark Pearson, Mary Kiefel, Emma, Karen lewis, Eddie Garcia, Caronda Bourgeois, David Humphries, Tracy Putland, Laura Monaghan, TheWeelou23, boy stio, Emily Haynes, Pam Brown, Sharon Campbell, Scott Menzies, Deirdre Gamill-Hock, Allison Valentine, Marika Borger, Joe Wardle, Kellie Collins, William Cahill, Candee Vaglica, Kristin Scearce, Lisa McGlade, Jay Evans, Janet Wilde, Mark Junk, Rafael Montes, Sarah Atherton, Trudy Bryan, Joanne Wheatley, John May, Stacie Jaye, Kirsty Mills, Louise, Kenneth Mcintire, Adam Thayer, Jonathan Emmerson, Susan Rowden, David Greer, Becki Sinks, Carole Wilson, Richard Sorden, Becki Battersby, Derek Titus, Phil, Clare Duncan, Julie Peacock, Rebecca Strouse, Stacie Denise, Sarah Powell, Paula Bruce, G. Stella, Michael J. Mulkerin, Sandra Lewis, Hawaii Lynn, Windi LaBounta, Stephanie Hardy, Janet Carter, Lisa Kruse, Gillian Adams, Lauren, Clare Lanes, Jacqueline Scifres, Cindy Ahlgren, John Best, Stacey Arkless, Nate Stephenson, Chris Jones, Jonathon & Tonia Cornell, Chris Hicks, Janine Hartley, Sandra Behrens, Carl Donze, Chris Nelson, Rigby Jackson, Linda Paisley, Karen Roethle, Carmen Hammond

CHAPTER ONE

EMILY WAS PULLING on her jacket, about to leave, when she heard the scream.

She hurried out of the stockroom and onto the shop floor, where she found her *Rube's News* coworker, Katie, clutching her left hand and shrieking like a wounded gazelle. Droplets of blood spattered the white vinyl tiles around her feet like a macabre art project.

Emily's heart caught in her throat. "What is it? What happened?"

"M-My hand! I cut myself." Katie was shaking like a leaf, her face devoid of colour as she stood in front of the humming drinks refrigerator. Several bottles of wine lay scattered at her feet. One of the bottles was broken, a bloody shard lying next to it in a pool of glistening alcohol.

"Okay, okay. It's okay!" Emily gathered Katie into her arms and tried to calm her by shushing and rocking her. "I got you, babes. You're all right. Let me see."

Katie tried to cling on, but Emily eased her back. She clutched her hand against her chest but offered it gingerly for inspection, closing her eyes and looking away.

Emily's stomach turned. *Oh God!*

Katie's palm had split in two. Pearls of pink-white tissue bulged around the wound's edge like uncooked sausage meat. Oddly, there was little blood, but the wound was undeniably deep.

She needs stitches. And vodka.

Emily glanced towards the cash register. It was nearly nine o'clock, so they had been about to close. Thankfully, there were no customers.

"What's all this racket?" John stormed out of the office, shoes clip-clopping on the tiles. When he saw the two of them huddled together by the refrigerator, his eyes narrowed behind his glasses and his upper lip curled upwards. "What are you two doing?"

Katie moaned. "I-I cut my hand."

"What? How?"

"I slipped. I-I was holding a bottle of wine and I landed—"

John glared at Emily, his unkempt eyebrows like two angry black caterpillars. "Why was the floor wet?"

She shrugged. *Why is he angry at me?* "I don't know. I was on my way out."

John elbowed her aside so that he could inspect Katie's palm. "Maybe if you'd been in less of a rush to leave, Emmie, this wouldn't have happened." She went to argue, to tell him it wasn't her fault, but he cut her off with a sharp hiss. "This is bad, Katie. We need to get you to A & E."

Katie panicked. "No, no, no."

Emily grabbed her by the shoulders and got her attention. She could smell the mint on her panicked breaths. "You'll be fine, Kat. Want me to come with you?"

Katie nodded, but John shook his head and moved Emily aside. "No. I'll take her, Emmie. You need to stay here and cash up for me."

"What? No, but I—"

John glared at her again, his eyes like saucers behind the thick lenses of his specs. "Will you stop thinking about yourself and be a team player for once? You don't have a car, do you? What are you planning to do? Take her on the bus? Look, I'll be back as soon as I can, okay?"

Katie snuffled, trying to keep from sobbing. "S-Sorry, Ems. I… I…"

Emily smiled to reassure her. "It's not your fault."

"Can I rely on you?" John asked her. He had his arm wrapped around Katie's shoulders, and his hand was inside the sleeve of her work shirt, touching the bare skin of her triceps. Emily had felt those same creeping fingers on her own flesh many a time. John had a way of brushing past you a little too closely, or giving you an encouraging pat on the lower back that sent a shiver up your spine. His aftershave smelled like cat litter, and his slicked-back brown hair glistened like he'd just got caught in the rain.

"Of course." Emily nodded. "Just take care of Katie."

"Good girl. I'll be back as soon as I can. And clean up that mess by the refrigerator."

She rolled her eyes. "Righto."

Emily watched the two of them disappear into the nearly night outside. The heavy fire door swished closed behind them, but not before a wave of muggy air blasted inside the shop.

She took off her jacket and draped it over the back of the swivel chair behind the cash register. Then she sat and commiserated with herself. Cashing up would take at least half an hour, and there were several end-of-day emails that needed to be sent to head office in Cambridge. After that, she would have to sit and wait for John to come back and set the alarm. She wasn't going home for a while.

This sucks. I've been here since noon.
It's not Katie's fault that she hurt herself. I hope she's okay.
But John can kiss my butt.

She reached into her jacket pocket and pulled out her phone. The cracked glass covering the display made her think about the broken wine bottle, and the pink, stringy flesh spilling out of Katie's palm. It made her shudder. Her coworker had clearly been in shock, but Emily realised now that she was pretty hyped up too. She took a moment to calm down, breathing steadily and rubbing her fingertips together. A self-caress.

Katie's going to have one hell of a scar.

I know from experience.

At six years old, Emily had fallen from a tree. That might have been bad enough, but she had landed on a muddy copper pipe that some previous kid must have been using to dig with. It had gone right up her shorts and torn a chunk out of her thigh. She still remembered – as if it were yesterday – racing home to her mum and screaming like the world was ending.

She spent three hours with me at the hospital and then we got ice cream.

The doctor said I was lucky it wasn't worse. I haven't climbed a tree since.

Emily opened up a message box on her phone and selected her best friend, Lily. She typed out a text: *Touchy Feely left me to close up. U will have to have fun without me :-(*

She pressed *send* and let out a sigh. Then she went and fetched a mop to clean Katie's blood up off the tiles.

Emily let out a sigh of relief when John returned at ten minutes past ten.

All the lights inside the shop were off except those at the front, creating a gloomy atmosphere that had been starting to freak her out. She'd cashed up the tills and locked the rear exits, so John just needed to set the alarm and lower the shutter. He stood now on the customer side of the checkout, leering at her through his glasses. "I'm sorry you had to stay late, Emmie. I'm grateful."

"It's fine. You weren't that long. How's Katie?"

"Getting stitches. Her mum's with her now."

Emily leant forward on the counter. "Bless her. I've been worried."

He reached across the counter and took her hand. "I'm sorry I yelled at you earlier. It's been a long day."

Ew! Don't touch me.

She pulled her hand back and folded her arms. She'd already put her jacket on, ready to leave. "Everything's done, so I'll see you Tuesday, yeah?"

The way he winced wasn't encouraging. "Actually, I'm going to need you to come in at ten tomorrow. Katie won't make the early shift now, so I'm going to be on my own."

"What? Oh, John, come on! I haven't had a day off since Sunday. I'm tired."

He shrugged as if it were out of his control. "I know, I know. Look, I'll make sure it's a nice easy shift, okay? There'll be a cup of coffee waiting for you first thing, and I'll stay on the shop floor with you all day."

She shuddered. *I'd rather you didn't.*

"I'm begging you, Emmie." He put his hands together in prayer. "I'm desperate."

Yeah, desperate is exactly how I'd describe you.

"Okay, fine." She deflated, and a heavy lump in her stomach made her want to lie down and moan. "But we need to get another member of staff, John. I'm only supposed to be doing thirty hours a week."

He reached over the counter again and this time clasped her elbow. "I promise, as soon as head office approves some extra hours in the budget, I'll take someone new on." He let go of her and stood back, fidgeting awkwardly with the silver cufflinks on his shirt cuffs. "So, um, what are you doing now? You need a lift home?"

"No!" She moved out from behind the counter and dodged past him, holding her breath to avoid sniffing in his stale aftershave. "The bus will only be a minute. I'll see you at ten."

"Or earlier, if you can make it."

"I'll do my best." She shoved open the door and stepped out into the balmy night. Summer was her favourite time of year, but hot nights could make sleeping a bitch. She feared hearing the birds chirping by the time she nodded off tonight.

I'm going to be exhausted.

She turned left and headed for the bus stop on the corner of Edward Street, but a voice called to her from the other side of the road. "Hey, Emmie! Where ya going?"

Emily frowned. Someone was standing in front of *Barney's Chippy*. It was almost dark out now, so the flickering marquee cast them in a ghostly orange light. "Lily? What are you doing?"

"Coming to get *you*, silly." She cupped a hand around her mouth as she shouted. "Did you think we were going to party without you?"

"Oh, babes. It's late and I have work in the morning." She glanced back at *Rube's*, making sure John wasn't stepping out behind her. "Touchy Feely sprung a shift on me."

Lily shouldered her handbag and trotted across the road. She'd added a pink streak to her black hair since they'd last seen each other, and a new nose stud glinted in the moonlight. "Screw him! Tomorrow's Sunday. You don't need to be in early, right?"

"Ten, but I'm exhausted. I told you to have fun without me."

Lily looped her arm around Emily's elbow and pulled her in the opposite direction she wanted to go. "We're not having a get-together without our little Emmie."

"Please don't call me that."

"Only if you come hang out."

Emily could feel her eyelids getting heavy, and she was still shaken by Katie's accident earlier. She just wanted to go home and sleep the day off. "I'm really not—"

"Matt's coming too. He's bringing Harry."

"What? Where?"

Lily smirked, her freckles peeking through the pale foundation she always slapped on a tad too thick. "They're meeting us at the Rock. Ross and Kaley are bringing the booze. Come on, girl. Just call in sick."

"I can't. John's on his own."

"So turn up with a hangover. You're doing him a favour, right? If he gives you shit, report him for groping you."

Emily glanced back again. John was still inside the shop, probably checking she'd cashed up properly. The guy didn't have a life. "He doesn't grope me, Lil. He's just... not good with boundaries."

"He's a disgusting perv and you should tell him where to go. How old is he, anyway? Forty?"

She shrugged. "Thirty-five, I think."

"Gross. Anyway, forget him." She winked. "Harry awaits."

She's not going to give up, is she?

I love her.

"Okay, okay." Emily put her hands up in surrender. "I'll hang out for an hour, but then I have to go get some sleep."

Lily hopped up and down, various chains attached to her clothing and canvass handbag jangling. About a year ago, she'd turned to the dark side, dying her brown hair black and piercing herself all over. Months had gone by since she'd worn shoes other than Doc Martens. Fortunately, she was still the same upbeat bestie she'd always been. "Let's get crunk, girl," she said in a Californian accent.

Emily rolled her eyes but couldn't keep from smiling. She stepped off the kerb to cross the road. "Calm down, Lil. I'm only going for—"

"Whoa!" Lily dragged her back onto the kerb just in time to avoid a speeding bus. The driver beeped his horn angrily. "Jesus, Ems! Watch where you're walking."

Emily grabbed her chest and gasped. "Holy shit! You just saved my life." Was lack of sleep now causing her to sleepwalk into traffic? "Like, literally!"

Lily looked like she was about to burst into tears. She shook her head, unblinking. "If I hadn't been looking... Fuck, that was so lucky."

"I think I need that drink now."

"Maybe make it two?"

Emily chuckled, her voice a little shaky. "Y-Yeah."

A beeping sound caused them to spin around. John was typing the alarm code into the panel.

Emily grabbed her friend by the arm. "Come on, Lil, before Touchy asks to join us."

"Ew, gross!"

They raced across the road, but this time Emily checked both ways.

I almost died!

CHAPTER
TWO

BOOLE-ON-SEA WAS A SHITTY TOWN, most residents would agree. It had one of the worst crime rates in the South East and one of the highest teen pregnancy rates. But it also had a kick-ass beach. A two-mile stretch of clean, protected sand with a raised promenade running alongside it and a small wooden pier at one end.

Emily loved the salty breeze that came off the sea at night. Even after having lived her entire life near the beach, she'd never fallen out of love with it. There was just something about staring off at the empty horizon that calmed her, made her feel insignificant – and her problems too. Sometimes she dreamed of saving up for a tiny sailboat and drifting away until she could no longer see land in any direction. No one to bother her. No one to pester her. Just the gentle swaying of the waves and the slosh of saltwater against the hull.

"Kaley texted me," said Lily, staring at her phone as they walked along the promenade. "They're already at the Rock."

The Rock was a stony outcropping separating Boole's beach into two sections: the upper beach and the lower beach. It was a good place to hang out at night because it kept your butt off the wet sand. The outcropping was also flat enough to make a pretty comfy seat. Although after a while your cheeks would get numb. The main reason they drank at the Rock during the summer months was because the pubs were rowdy, with obnoxious holidaymakers desperate to make the most of their nights.

Emily saw her friend's silvery silhouettes come into view. The moon was full, and it allowed her to see all the way out to the distant sea. The tide would be out now until sunrise, and an army of gulls assaulted the vast stretch of wet sand, pecking at defenceless cockles and stranded shore crabs. Along with the overflowing bins outside *Barney's* chip shop, the local birds never lacked for food.

Kaley waved when she saw Emily. Ross wolf-whistled. It'd been two weeks since they'd all got together like this. She sometimes met up with Lily during the week, but rarely with the others. Kaley was at the University of Essex always studying, and Ross worked long hours at his family's Cantonese restaurant – they were from Hong Kong originally but had given their son an English name since he'd been born here. Lily worked at a fancy salon.

Harry was a friend of Matt, both of them apprentices at the same garage. Emily had known Matt since middle school, but she had only met Harry once or twice. He was six feet tall, though, and extremely handsome – and she'd always had a thing for blond guys.

And bad boys. Love me a bad boy.

Along with Lily, Emily hopped over the low stone wall running alongside the promenade. The two of them then dangled by their fingertips before kicking off and dropping onto the wet sand six feet below. Their twin landings caused a nearby gull to flap its wings irritably.

Harry immediately came over and handed Emily a bottle of vodka mixed with Red Bull. A nice glass of wine in a restaurant was more her style, but she was happy to slum it for a night.

Not exactly a queue of guys waiting to take me out to dinner. Other than John. Ew!

"Thanks." She took a swig and gasped; there was more vodka than Red Bull. "Yikes!"

Harry chuckled and raised an eyebrow. It had a slit in it, which was pretty retro, but somehow he pulled it off. His light blue eyes added a great deal to his attractiveness. "I'm glad you came. Lily said your dickhead of a boss made you work late."

"Girl I work with had an accident. There wasn't much of a choice."

"For real? What happened?"

"She cut her hand open on some glass. It was pretty gross to be honest."

He took the bottle back from her and swigged from it. "Well, I'm glad you made it. You can relax now."

"Yeah, that's the plan." Emily realised she was smiling like a dork, so she distracted herself by clambering up onto the Rock to join Kaley and Ross. Halfway up, she lost her footing, which she thought she'd got away with until Matt gave a cheer.

"Nice one, Ems!"

"Get knotted!" She could already feel her cheeks getting red as she reached out to take Kaley's hand and hoist herself up onto the outcropping.

Kaley smirked at her. "Long time no see. How are things?"

Emily shuffled onto her butt. "Same as ever. I'm single, broke, and I hate my job. How about you?"

"I'm all right. I have some exams coming up, but I think I'm ready for them."

"I can't believe you're going to be a lawyer."

"A solicitor, but that's still a couple of years away."

"The way your mum goes on, you'd think you were already a judge."

"She's Sikh. I'm not a daughter; I'm a bludgeon to beat her rivals with." She shook her head and tittered. "I can't even remember whether it was me who wanted to study law or her."

"Pretty sure it was her," said Emily. "You were always into art when we were kids."

Kaley grinned. "Oh yeah. Can you remember those comics I used to draw?"

"Queen Boomerang? Of course, I do. She was cool."

"Oh my God, I forgot about her. She was going to change the world for the better with her powers. I used to dream I was her."

"You will be one day, I'm sure. You've always wanted to help people in need."

She nodded. "Yeah, that's why I'm friends with Ross."

Ross was sitting on Kaley's other side. He elbowed her in the ribs and then waved at Emily. "Hiya, Ems."

"Hey, Ross. How's the restaurant?"

"Hot! I hate being in the kitchen when the weather's stuffy like this."

"I keep telling him to quit," said Kaley, shaking her head. "Do something he actually wants to do."

Ross shrugged. "I don't mind it. It's better than earning minimum wage working for someone else, ain't it?"

Emily grunted. "Yeah, I don't recommend it."

"Sorry. I just mean I'm lucky my family owns a business. It has its pros."

She waved a hand dismissively. "I'm not offended. My job sucks. In fact, every job I've ever had has sucked. Problem is, I'm not good at anything like you guys. I guess I haven't figured it out yet." She shrugged. "You know, life?"

"You'll get there." Kaley patted her on the knee. "Not everyone has pushy parents like us, directing their entire lives. You're lucky in a way."

"Lucky, yeah, right. Or it could just be that I'm meant for menial retail jobs and no love life."

"No way," said Ross. "You're one of the most awesome people I know, Ems. You're going to be fine, I promise. You'll figure things out."

She winked at him. "Thanks, babes."

"No problem." He got up from the Rock and patted down

his backside. "I'm gonna stretch my legs. I'm getting butt cramp."

Kaley whacked him on the rump and made him yelp. "Sorry," she said. "Just trying to get your blood flowing again."

"Um, thanks."

As Ross climbed down to join the boys, Lily climbed up to join the girls. She reached out a hand, prompting Kaley to pass her an alcopop from a cardboard box beside her. She popped the cap with a bottle opener attached to a chain on her handbag.

"You're like Inspector Gadget," said Emily, and she reached back to pull the band from her ponytail so she could retie it tighter. Strands of blonde hair came loose and floated in front of her face.

"Who?"

"That cartoon geezer with the arms."

"Never heard of him, babes."

Emily rolled her eyes. "It don't matter. Hand me a drink."

Lily popped the lid on a second bottle and handed it over. It was sickly sweet, and the bubbles burned her throat as she swallowed, but the warmth spread through her thighs almost immediately. It'd been a while since she'd last drank, and it felt good.

I just wish I didn't have work in the morning. Screw you, John.

Lily caught Emily's attention with a smirk. "So you gonna make a move on Harry tonight, babes?" She nodded towards the boys below, who were sniggering about something.

"What? No way."

"Why not?"

"Because…"

"Because you're a timid little mouse?" Lily put on a kiddy voice. "And the thought of kissing a boy makes your fanny flutter?"

Emily groaned. "You're so gross." She raised the bottle to her lips but didn't drink yet. "I just want to see what happens. I'm still getting to know him." She took a swig.

"He's hot," said Kaley. "What's to know?"

Lily nodded in agreement, her multiple earrings glinting in the moonlight. "Exactly. I mean, I prefer my men short and chubby with bad skin, but I suppose Harry would do in a pinch. Look, if you're too scared to act on it, babes, I'll help you." She put her hands to her mouth and hollered. "Hey, Harry?"

Harry turned around. "Yeah, Lil? What's up?"

Emily glared at her. "Don't you dare! If you say something, I'll never talk to you again."

Lily side-eyed Emily and smirked. "Um... don't get too wasted, yeah? We need you to drive us all home later."

"I'm fine," said Harry, scrunching up his face. "I can drink all night and still drive straight."

Ross cleared his throat. He was holding the bottle of vodka Red Bull, but he wasn't drinking it. "I might get a taxi. You want to go twos, Ems?"

Emily nodded. She and Ross lived pretty close to each other, although his house was far nicer than the one she shared with her mum. "Sure. Sounds good."

"I'll take everyone home," said Harry, a little peevishly. "Don't waste your money."

"Yeah," said Matt, his hands buried deep in his pockets while he waited for the bottle to make its way back around to him. His brown hair had grown longer and flapped in the breeze. "It'll be fine."

Ross appeared uncomfortable, but he didn't argue. Neither did Emily, although she was reluctant to get in a car with a drunk driver. Even a cute one.

Lily reached over and nudged Emily. "Ross is trying to get you to himself, girl."

"Lucky cow," said Kaley, pulling her knees up against her chest and tapping her half-empty bottle rhythmically against her shin. "He never even notices me."

"Huh?" Emily cocked her head. "You like Ross? Since when?

Isn't he, like, a brother to you?"

"Ew, gross. No, he's just... we get along, you know? He's chill. Anyway, he clearly likes you."

"No, he don't!"

Lily swigged from her bottle and burped. Then she wiped her mouth and tutted. "He totally does, Ems. He's been into you for like a year, now. Hey, maybe you, him, and Harry can have a *ménage à trois*."

Kaley cackled.

"You two are acting like teenagers. How much have you drunk?"

"Only a bottle," said Lily. "Or four."

"You're gonna be fucked."

Lily swigged from her bottle again. "Here's hoping. I can't remember the last time I had a good orgas—"

Kaley yelped. For a moment it was unclear why, but then Lily howled with laughter. "Oh, he got you good!"

A seagull had swooped overhead and dropped a bomb – resulting in a direct hit. A great white splotch now covered the shoulder of Kaley's red leather jacket, and gritty bits glistened in her jet-black hair. She shook her head and groaned. "Please tell me that's not what I think it is."

"Hold on," said Lily, trying to keep from laughing. "I've got some wipes in my handbag."

Emily had to laugh as well. It was contagious. "Hey, don't worry about it. It's supposed to be lucky."

"I don't feel lucky. I feel like I'm covered in bird shit."

"Lucky bird shit."

Lily handed Kaley a wipe from her bag and helped her clean herself up, while Emily sipped from her bottle and enjoyed the warmth of the night and the alcohol. For a while she'd been on a treadmill of mundanity – work, sleep, work, sleep – so it was nice to be irresponsible for a change. The only bad part was that she knew she would be right back on that treadmill tomorrow.

"Hey," Harry called up from the sand. He had something in

his hand, a tiny see-through plastic bag. "Want to take things up a notch? I have happiness to share."

"You brought Es?" Lily's eyes went wide. "Oh hell yeah!" She turned to Kaley. "You in?"

Kaley shrugged. "I got nowhere to be."

Harry handed a pill to Matt, who swallowed it without hesitation. Ross did the same, which was surprising since he was usually the group's voice of reason. Harry must have already talked both of them into it.

"Not for me," said Emily. "I have work."

I hate you, John.

Harry pulled a face. "Call in sick. It's only a job."

"She can't!" Lily spoke in a tone that was a little unkind. "Her pervy boss wants her all to himself. He'll be heartbroken if she skives off."

Emily frowned. "Hey, I told you I was only coming for a few drinks. Why are you being so harsh?"

Lily gave her a playful shove. "Oh, come on. When did you last let your hair down? You're always working in that crappy little shop. John'll have to figure something out."

"Just drink a load of water before you go to bed," said Matt. "I've gone to work on zero sleep plenty of times before. It's fine once you get a few coffees in you."

"I don't know…"

Harry moved to the bottom of the Rock and peered up at her. "Please, Ems? I'll be gutted if you leave."

"Really?"

"Yeah, of course. I wanted to hang out tonight." He popped a pill in his mouth and swallowed. "I'll take care of you. I promise."

Emily closed her eyes for a moment and tried to gauge her tiredness. When she struggled to open them again, she realised it was bordering on exhaustion. Which was what made it a surprise when she said yes.

I'm going to regret this.

But Lil's right. Screw John.

"Okay, I'll take one." She climbed down onto the sand. "But I'm blaming you for whatever happens."

Harry grinned and handed her a tiny pill. He then glanced over her shoulder, up towards Kaley. "Hey, are you... are you covered in bird shit?"

"Yeah." Kaley groaned. "Lucky bird shit, apparently."

They all started laughing.

For ten minutes, Emily didn't feel a thing. Then she felt a little odd. Finally, she felt fucking great. Her weariness evaporated and suddenly nothing in the world mattered. She was with friends and all was fantastic. She almost wished she hadn't sneakily bitten her pill in half and spat a portion onto the sand.

I couldn't fully let go. Why am I like that?

What am I scared of?

"Hey," said Lily, jangling one of her chains that hung from her jeans pocket. "I want to walk. Can we go for a walk? Just along the beach? Come on."

"All right," said Harry. "I'm down with that."

"Me too," said Emily, unable to control her mad grinning. "Let's walkety walk, walk, walk."

And so they did.

They strolled along the wet sand for twenty minutes or an hour... or a full week – Emily had no idea, but it was lovely. Lily linked arms with her and they sang songs from the *Trolls* soundtrack, ordering everyone else to join in. Kaley had her arm around Ross's waist, leaning against him as they walked. Harry and Matt roughhoused, trying to trip each other over on the sand. A balmy Saturday night, and for once Emily was enjoying herself.

"I'd best text my mum," she said, pulling out her phone. "She'll be worried about me. Shit! It's past eleven already."

"Time flies," said Kaley, but she didn't complete the phrase.

It took several attempts, but Emily sent off a text saying she was with Lily and would be home late. Her mum replied within seconds, telling her to be safe.

"I'm always safe," she said out loud.

Lily looked at her. "Huh?"

"Nothing. Hey, Lil?"

"What?"

"You're my bestie."

Lily squeezed her. "Love you, Emmie."

"Don't call me that. I'll bite you."

"I'll bite you back! I could eat you all up."

"Like vanilla… or maybe custard. Hey, can we go for a walk?"

"We are walking," said Harry.

"Oh yeah. Ha!"

They walked a while longer, this stretch in silence. A mournful howl came in off the sea and kept them from talking. They'd brought booze along with them, but Emily's mouth felt like she'd been tonguing a camel's arsehole, and she wished for some water. The last thing she wanted was to work all day tomorrow with a pounding skull.

Don't think about work. It'll send you on a downer.

Matt fell down in the sand as Harry tripped him. "You dickhead," he said as he rose to his knees and wiped sand off his hands. "Stupid prick."

Harry helped him back up. "Sorry, geez. You all right?"

"Yeah." Matt brushed the back of his legs, then tried to launch a surprise attack.

Harry dodged and tripped him over again. "Nice try, mate."

Matt grumbled and got back to his feet, his brown hair a mess on his forehead. "Dickhead."

"Don't fight," said Ross. "It always ends up getting out of hand."

"We're only messing around," said Harry. "Chill."

Matt nodded in agreement, but he was huffing and puffing,

and both his fists were clenched by his sides. He and Harry had come to blows before, often vying to be the alpha of the group, but most of the time it was harmless. Sometimes, though, Matt seemed to regret having brought Harry into their group.

Emily rolled her eyes. *Boys. I still remember when Matt used to tell everyone at school that he was a black belt. The kids believed it, too, until the day Che Gibbs offered to fight him on the rugby field.*

Kaley was standing next to Ross, but she broke away now to point a finger ahead. "Hey, there are people dossing under the pier."

Emily put a hand over her eyes and squinted. It made her feel like a sailor on a deck and she giggled at herself. About a hundred metres up the beach, Boole Pier stretched out over the sand. Beneath it, leaning against the wood and steel struts, were half a dozen individuals. Small beads of light highlighted cigarettes being passed back and forth, and the faint sound of laughter suggested it was a group of young people chilling.

"Probably kids," said Kaley. "Out past their bedtime."

"Maybe," said Harry. "Let's go check it out. Might be a laugh."

Emily groaned. She was feeling good, but she wasn't in the mood for socialising. In fact, she wasn't even sure if she could manage a conversation with her sticky lips and dry tongue. "Can't we just go chill at the bandstand, or head back to the Rock?"

Harry turned and took her hand. It sent an excited shiver up her spine. "We're only going to say hello, babes. See what's up, yeah? They might be cool."

Emily looked down. He was definitely holding her hand. "I just like it being us."

"Me too. Maybe we can go off for a chat later?"

"I'd like that."

His piercing blue eyes seemed to glow in the dark as he peered at her. "You're so beautiful."

She tucked a loose strand of hair behind her ear and looked away. "I'm really not."

"Why do you do that? Why are you so down on yourself?"

"I dunno." She shrugged. "I'm just—"

"Come on!" said Matt. "Are we going or not?"

Harry raised an eyebrow at her questioningly. "You game?"

She nodded, so they carried on along the beach, holding hands. Ross glanced at them, and she wondered if she saw jealousy in his expression.

No way does Ross like me. We've known each other since we were kids. He was at my tenth birthday party and threw up from too much cake.

The thought of having two lads interested in her was ridiculous. Lily was far prettier – underneath all the goth make-up – and Kaley's mocha skin was flawless. If anything, Emily was the ugly duckling of the group.

But Harry was holding *her* hand.

He's high. He might not even remember tomorrow.

Emily didn't know how long ago she'd taken the E, but she felt a little less floaty now. Her calves were aching from walking in the wet sand and the salty air was stinging her eyes.

Should I ask for another pill?

No. I don't want to end up wrecked.

She swigged the last of her alcopop and held the empty bottle in her free hand. Kaley and Lily had finished theirs, too. Matt held the bottle of vodka Red Bull. It was almost all gone.

They approached the people under the pier. Boole was a small town, so there was always a chance of bumping into someone you knew, but once they got closer, the people revealed themselves to be strangers.

"Aight, geez," said Harry, calling out. The strangers were men, five of them, of a similar age to Emily's group – early twenties. They each sported neatly trimmed black beards and thick eyebrows.

"Hello," said one of the young men with an accent. He wore

a black vest and had a jumper tied around his waist. "Can we help you?"

Harry's grip tightened on Emily's hand. "Just being friendly, mate, innit?"

"Okay." The young man took a drag on his cigarette and nodded. "Good to meet you then."

"Nice night, huh?"

"A blessed night."

"So you one of them over from Albania, are ya? Came over in a dinghy from France?"

Lily chuckled and so did Matt, but Ross pulled a face that suggested he was less amused by the sudden, unwarranted accusation.

The young man dropped his cigarette stub onto the sand and stomped it out. "What? Albania?"

"Yeah," said Harry, speaking slowly. "Are. You. From. Fucking. Albania?"

"No. I am from Syria. We are all from Syria. *Ahlan.*"

Harry nodded as if satisfied, but the words that came out of his mouth spoke differently. "No fucking better, is it? What you doing here?"

The Syrian was about to answer, but one of his companions pushed him aside. This man was larger, with a pointy beard jutting off his chin like a spike. He wore a long, flowing T-shirt over a pair of ripped jeans. "Why don't you go away? We are not doing any trouble."

Harry looked at Emily and smirked. "You hear this guy? Can barely speak English."

"Just leave it," she said, trying to pull him away. "Let's go back to the Rock."

Is he trying to start a fight? Why?

Harry glared at the stranger. "I want to hang out here, Ems. Why should we be the ones to leave?"

"They were here first."

"No." He shook his head at her. "We were."

"What is problem?" asked pointy-beard. His dark eyelashes were feminine, but the rest of his face was angular and harsh. "Why are you angry?"

Harry let go of Emily's hand and fronted up to him. "Because you shouldn't be here, mate, that's why. I'm sick of this country being invaded. Royal Navy should shoot your sodding dinghies out of the water."

"We have done nothing to you. Leave us."

"*You* leave. This is *my* country."

"Yeah," said Lily. "Just go. You're not welcome here."

Emily gasped. "Lily?"

"What? Everyone is sick of it, Ems. Boole is overrun with illegal immigrants."

Ross nodded at the Syrian, not confrontationally, but more curious. "*Did* you come here illegally?"

The smaller man, the one in the black vest, cleared his throat. Rather than a full beard, he had a neatly shaped goatee. "What does it matter? We are here now, and all we want is a safe place to live and work."

Harry sneered. "You mean you have ten kids and claim benefits for them all?"

"Fucking parasites," said Matt. His fists clenched as he moved beside Harry.

Emily shook her head, trying to figure out what the hell was happening. Her friend's eyes were like big black holes, and their jaws jutted out as if they'd become detached. They were high, and drunk, and saying things they probably would be ashamed of otherwise.

Or is this what they really think?

I don't like this.

"Can we go?" She tried to get Harry's attention, but he ignored her. She ended up making eye contact with the black-vested young man, and they shared a moment where it became clear they were both on the same page. Neither of them wanted trouble.

But Harry did.

"This is our pier," he said, pointing a finger at pointy-beard. "Leave."

Pointy-beard took a step closer to Harry, puffing out his chest. "Who will make us?"

"I will, you prick."

"Come on," said Kaley. "This isn't worth it."

"Calm down, Samaan," said his friend. "Do not rise to temper."

"Let's just go," said Ross.

Pointy-beard nodded. "Listen to your Chinese friend. Or does he not belong here either?"

"My grandparents came here legally," said Ross testily. The comment seemed to rile him. "We're not the same."

"Yeah," said Harry. "Ross's family was welcomed here. Same goes for Kaley's family. I ain't got a problem with foreigners who come here the right way, respecting our way of life. My problem is with scum like you who come to take advantage. Piss off back to Albania, mate."

Pointy-beard rolled his eyes. "Get out of my face, stupid boy."

"Who you calling a boy, mate?"

Emily reached out to Harry. "This is ridiculous. Let's just calm down and—"

Harry threw a punch. It landed with a horrible, fleshy *whap!*

Pointy-beard had a few inches on Harry, but he staggered backwards in shock. His friends tried to catch him, but he flopped onto the sand. Harry immediately leapt forward and planted a kick in the side of his head.

Lily cheered.

Emily felt sick. "Stop it! Please!"

Ross tried to pull Harry back, but he was like a wild animal. He wouldn't stop. He kicked pointy-beard again, in the ribs, and forced the air out of him in a pained gasp.

The man's friends cried out in horror and ran to his aid.

"Samaan, are you okay?" one of them said. "Are you hurt?" asked another. Harry threw punches at them all.

The black-vested young man shook his head at Emily, his dark eyes full of hurt and accusation. "Why do you do this? Why?"

"I…" Before she could answer, someone punched Ross in the mouth and dropped him.

Matt roared in anger and smashed the vodka bottle over a stranger's head.

Then all hell broke loose.

CHAPTER
THREE

ROSS DROPPED onto the sand like a sack of potatoes. Emily didn't think she'd ever seen him in a fight before, and the punch seemed to shock him more than it hurt. Kaley immediately went berserk, throwing herself at the man who had assaulted him and spitting obscenities. She clawed at his face, kicked at his legs. "Fucking animal. *Dafa ho!*"

Matt tossed the broken vodka bottle and moved to fight side by side with Harry, who was swinging at the strangers like a lunatic. Nearby, a young man lay on the sand, clutching his badly bleeding head and moaning. A wide, red gash glistened beneath his dark hair.

Emily stood frozen in disbelief at what was happening. The empty alcopop bottle fell from her hand and thudded in the sand. Whatever buzz had remained was now gone. She was completely sober – and aghast as she watched Lily join the battle, her friend of umpteen years, who had never even crushed a spider.

What is she doing? Has she lost her mind?

The only two not embroiled in violence were Emily and the lad in the black vest. He looked as horrified as her but had the added defence of being innocent. Harry had started this. These young men had been doing nothing except minding their own business.

"Stop it," she muttered, shaking her head. "Stop it."

But the fight continued, fists and feet flying. It was a clumsy battle that quickly descended into a shoving match. Pointy-beard was still lying on the ground. His mouth was bloody, and he clutched at his ribs. The young man who Matt had hit with the bottle was dragging himself away through the wet sand like a slug.

Feeling traitorous, Emily moved away from her friends and rushed over to pointy-beard, crouching beside him to check if he was okay.

But he swatted her aside. "Get away from me, woman."

"I'm sorry. I just want to help."

A hand on Emily's shoulder startled her. She looked up and saw black vest. "Get your friends away from here," he warned her. "Please."

Emily yelped as the wounded man lashed out at her again. "Dante! Get her away from me."

Black vest – Dante – reached out to her, but Emily dodged away. Her hands rose in surrender. "I'm just trying to help."

"Then leave," he said. "You are bad people."

"No… No, we're not. We're…"

Harry broke through the crowd and kicked pointy-beard yet again, this time in the side of his thigh. He howled and rolled to his feet, anger helping him regain strength. He raised a fist at Harry, but Emily leapt in his way, cowering. "Please stop!"

Finally, they heard her.

Everyone was huffing and puffing, but they stepped away from each other.

Pointy-beard clutched his ribs, struggling to breathe. Through bleeding lips, his words came out forcefully. "We come here to live in peace. Away from war and rape and murder. But this place... it is no better." He looked over at his friend with the bleeding head. "The people of this country are barbarians."

"Fuck you," said Harry. "We don't want you here. You're not welcome. Do you hear me? Not welcome. The rest of you can drown in the Channel for all I care. Your women and children too!"

Emily shook her head. "Harry! What the hell?"

Pointy-beard's expression darkened. While he'd been angry before, he was enraged now. Slowly, he lifted a finger and pointed at Harry, then glared at each of them in turn – including Emily. He said something in words she couldn't understand – Arabic, maybe – and she made out guttural sounds like *klanek* and *abhub*. His gaze was full of rage. Full of hate.

Dante shook his head. He said something to his friend but went ignored. After a moment, his gaze fell upon Emily again. "I'm sorry," he said. "I am very sorry."

Emily frowned. "For what? Why are you sorry?"

"Come on," said Harry, smirking like a cat eyeing a mouse. "I think we made our point. Let's leave these rats to lick their wounds." He pointed at pointy-beard, who was still muttering in a foreign language, almost chanting now. "And if I see you at this pier again, I'll kill you."

Pointy-beard ignored him and continued chanting. He had closed his eyes and no longer seemed to be listening.

Dante reached out and touched Emily on her arm. His touch was gentle. "Take your friends away from here," he said. "And... good luck."

Emily wanted to ask him what he meant, but Harry grabbed her wrist painfully and yanked her away. She tried to protest, but she was too confused – too dazed by what had just happened. The way Lily and Kaley whooped and cackled as they skipped down the beach disgusted her. They were acting like racist thugs.

But they're my best friends.

What the hell?

They were halfway back to the Rock when Emily stopped to puke. Her head was spinning and there was a sharp pain in her chest. For a moment, she thought she might pass out. Harry stood beside her, rubbing her back. "You're okay, babes. I got you."

"What the fuck was that?" She spat tangy phlegm onto the sand. "What is wrong with you?"

Harry recoiled. "What? Those vermin shouldn't be here. We have a right to defend our shores."

"Yeah," said Matt.

Emily wiped her mouth with the back of her hand. It should've mortified her to puke in front of him, but she was too angry to give a shit. "They weren't hurting anyone. They were just hanging out and smoking. You broke a bottle over that lad's head, Matt. Who the hell are you?"

All he could do was shrug and turn away.

Lily pulled a face. "Come on, Ems. Illegal immigrants are costing this country an arm and a leg. I agree we shouldn't have got into a fight with them, but still…" She shrugged. "They're not exactly innocent."

Harry nodded. "Most of 'em come here to join gangs."

"Not Syrians," said Ross. "It's the Eastern Europeans who join gangs."

Emily put her hands on her head. "Who the hell cares? When was the last time any of us were attacked by Eastern Europeans? Has anyone lost their job because of an illegal immigrant? The world isn't perfect, sure, but we just assaulted a group of people minding their own business. We weren't defending our shores – whatever that even means – and we weren't the good guys. That was so fucked up, guys."

Kaley pinched the bridge of her nose and groaned. "You're

right. I... I only got involved because they hit Ross. It triggered me."

Ross moaned. His left eye was puffy. "He sucker-punched me."

"I know," said Kaley, smiling weakly at him. "You did fine, babes."

Harry put his hands on his hips and started pacing up and down the beach. A slight breeze lifted his blond hair away from his face. "I lost my head, I admit it, but we've all had a drink and popped some pills." He moved in front of Emily and grabbed both her hands as he looked at her. "That wasn't me, Ems. It's just... I get so wound up sometimes at the state of this country. My dad tells me how people used to be proud to be British. It meant something. Now we let people take the piss, and we're too nice to do anything about it. Don't you ever worry about where we're heading?"

Emily sighed. She was exhausted again and desperate for bed. "Of course I worry. I worry about a lot of things – and yes, that includes illegal immigration. But beating people up... It makes me feel sick. You acted like an animal, Harry."

"We're all high," said Lily, running her ringed fingers through her shiny black hair. "You know me, Ems. I wouldn't hurt a fly."

Kaley nodded. "I reckon we're getting too old for popping pills. It ain't fun any more." She dropped onto her butt and reached for her trainers. "God, my feet are killing me. How far did we walk tonight?"

Harry was staring at his knuckles, turning them back and forth in front of him. Then he looked at her again. "How can I make this okay, Ems?"

"You can't. It's done."

He stared at her with those light blue eyes; so much sadness in them. "I'm so sorry. I really blew it, didn't I?"

She couldn't bear his pitiful stare, so she let out a sigh and tried to smile. "It's fine. Just don't do anything like that ever again. I hate violence, Harry. Hate it!"

"I promise I'll never do anything like that again." He let his head hang. "I'll make it up to you."

Matt let out a chuckle, seemingly in a world of his own.

Emily turned and frowned at him. "What's funny?"

"That geezer... What the hell was he saying to us?" He squinted and pointed a finger at them, mumbling a load of nonsense and trying to imitate pointy-beard's bizarre chant.

Lily started laughing. "I think he put a pox on us."

"They have old-fashioned ways in the Middle East," said Ross. "He was probably trying to make us infertile."

"He was speaking Arabic," said Kaley. "I didn't understand most of it. Sounded a bit like a prayer."

"Yep," said Matt, smirking. "The bugger cursed us for sure. Harry's dick's going to shrivel up and drop off any minute now. Look, you can tell it's already shrinking."

Everyone laughed, except for Emily. The way pointy-beard had glared at them all had been disturbing, but something else had worried her more: the expression on Dante's face. He'd been horrified by whatever his friend was saying. Why?

And what did he say to me before we left?

Good luck.

"I want to go home now, guys." Emily checked her watch. "God, it's almost midnight. If I get back now, I can still get a decent sleep before work."

Matt huffed. "You're still going in?"

"I don't want the hassle of calling in sick. I feel okay – just a bit shaken up – so I'm just going to drink a load of water and go to bed."

Lily sighed. "I'm sorry tonight got ruined, babes. Forgive me?"

Emily hugged her. "It's fine. But like Kaley said, I think we're too old for drugs."

"Life ends at twenty-two, huh? That sucks."

Harry ran a hand along Emily's shoulder and made her shiver. "Come on, I'll drive everyone back. The fight sobered me up."

Emily stared at him. His pupils were more their normal size now, and his jaw was almost in the right place. Truthfully, she didn't have the strength to argue, nor the patience to wait for a taxi, so despite her better judgement, she agreed to go with him. "You better concentrate on the road, or I'll make that eye even worse."

He frowned and put a hand to his face. He obviously hadn't realised he'd been punched. The bottom of his left eye was dark and swollen. It made him and Ross look like twins. "Ouch! Bugger must have clocked me one."

Emily gave him a little shove. "You deserved it. Maybe you'll think twice next time."

"I promise to behave." He reached down and took her hand. "Come on. Let's get you to bed."

"You wish!" She couldn't help but smirk. *God help me, but I really do like a bad boy.*

But not as bad as he's been tonight.

Ross helped Kaley up off the sand. She'd taken off her trainers and socks and now held them in her hands as she walked. After four or five steps, she fell back down, screaming.

Ross panicked, hopping back and forth. "What? What happened?"

Kaley clutched her foot and hissed. "I stepped on something. Shit, it hurts."

Emily broke away from Harry and knelt beside her friend. There was a seashell half-buried in the sand, its curved, spiky edge glinting like a razor-blade. It had sliced the sole of Kaley's foot wide open. Blood oozed everywhere.

Jesus! First Katie at work, now Kaley?

"It really hurts. I don't think I can walk on it. Motherfucker!"

"Maybe that bird shit wasn't so lucky after all," said Matt, and then he grimaced. "Sorry."

Ross put a hand to his mouth. "That looks bad, Kay."

"Really bad," said Harry, wrinkling his nose.

Kaley threw back her head and groaned. She was already turning pale. They needed to take care of her.

Emily put a hand to her face and closed her eyes, wishing she'd gone straight home after work.

CHAPTER
FOUR

"IT HURTS," said Kaley, and she unleashed a torrent of foul language. When she was angry, she took on a Punjabi lilt that was usually charming. Now it was a little scary. She was hopping on one foot, propped up by Matt and Ross. Blood dripped from her foot. "*Behenchod*! It hurts."

Emily shivered. It was midnight, and the balmy night had finally turned brisk. She wished more and more for her bed – and a pint glass full of water. Tonight had been a bad idea; one she would pay for in the morning.

Maybe I should just quit. It would be worth it just to shaft John.

No. Without a job, my life would be even more pathetic.

They helped Kaley up over the low stone wall and onto the concrete promenade. Lily held her shoes, following along behind and looking a little worse for wear. They were all coming down now, their faces sagging and their movements clumsy.

"I'm parked over by the Co-op," said Harry, manoeuvring Kaley towards the crossing. "How are you doing, Kay?"

"I'm great," she said, her arm around his neck. "Most fun I've had in years."

"You should go to the hospital," said Emily. "You might need stitches." *She definitely needs stitches.*

"I'm not spending hours in A & E with all the drunks."

Matt nodded. "It's just a gash. You'll be fine."

"What do you know about gash, mate?" said Harry.

Lily chuckled. "That's gross."

"Yeah," said Emily. "Gross."

"Sorry."

They crossed the road in a disorderly gaggle. At this time of night, the only cars on the road were the odd taxi taking people home from the pubs, of which there were almost a dozen in the town centre, mostly concentrated around the pier. This part of the seafront was quieter, full of charity shops and pop-up businesses that were all closed at night. Half the units were empty, like on most of Britain's high streets.

They made it onto the pavement and started towards the Co-op supermarket at the end of the road. Emily had worked there for a few months but had quit after failing to integrate with a clique of young girls already there. Lily had called them the Co-op-Cunts, which Emily had found to be a little crass, but it hadn't stopped her from giggling every time she heard it.

"What a night," said Ross, rubbing at his blackening eye. "Not looking forward to explaining this to my dad. I'm supposed to be on front of house tomorrow night."

"Just tell him you walked into a door," said Matt.

"Yeah right. I couldn't even convince him I was ill when I was dying of appendicitis. I doubt he'll believe I got a black eye from a door."

"At least the other guy came off worse," said Harry, but when he caught Emily's disapproving glare, he cleared his throat and looked away. "Not that it matters."

"We're lucky it wasn't worse," she said, hating that she was being so nagging, but unable to just go with the flow of causal violence. "Someone could've been really hurt."

"You're right," said Harry. He adjusted his grip on Kaley, which caused her to swear. "I totally agree."

They shuffled along for a few more minutes, Kaley panting with the exertion of having to hop on one leg. Her foot left bloody droplets on the pavement behind her, but it was slowly stopping. Hopefully, the wound wasn't as bad as it had seemed.

Something moved up ahead. A black cat. Emily only recognised it because of its unmistakably feline eyes that glinted in the darkness. It crouched beneath a ladder propped up against one of the buildings – a risky thing to leave out in Boole, seeing as people would steal the chewing gum right out of your mouth if you weren't paying attention. When the cat saw them coming, it scampered across the road and hopped the stone wall onto the beach below. A moment later, a pair of seagulls took flight, giving an irritated *haw-haw-haw*.

Lily stepped onto the road to avoid the ladder, but Matt and Harry carried Kaley right underneath it. Emily felt a pit grow in her stomach, but she ignored it. Superstitions were stupid, she knew that, and yet…

She called out to Ross as he approached the ladder. "Hey, it's bad luck to walk beneath a ladder."

Ross didn't seem to hear her, or he didn't get that she was talking to him, so he walked right underneath the ladder. On the other side, he stopped and turned to face her. "You what, Ems?"

"I said…" She shook her head. "Nothing. It doesn't matter."

She stepped around the ladder, not willing to tempt fate herself, and then she walked beside Ross. He smiled glumly at her. "Sorry I got involved earlier. I should've done more to stop it."

"I'm just going to put it down to drugs and alcohol."

"Yeah, me too. I love this country, and part of that is because it accepts everyone. I wouldn't be here if it didn't."

Emily grabbed his hand and squeezed. "I'm glad you're here. Let's just forget about it. I know you're not violent, Ross."

He nodded, but he still seemed upset about something. "Ems? Can I ask you a question?"

"Oh…" She had a bad feeling. "Sure, what is it?"

Overhead, the gulls were still flapping about in the sky, still irritated by having been disturbed by the black cat. They flew off towards the rooftops of the buildings alongside the road.

"I just wanted to ask you if…" He started again, swallowing a lump in his throat. "Look, I know you're like—"

There was a sudden squawk from above. One of the gulls had seemingly been startled by something. Next came a strange shuffling sound, like something sliding down a rough slope.

Emily and Ross looked up at the same time. A black shape moved through the air. Not a seagull.

"Look out!" Her warning was too late. The falling object struck Ross right in the centre of his face. The thud was sickening, and it was followed by a second impact as he collapsed and struck his head on the pavement.

Lily turned around and yelped. "Ross?"

He was out cold, his face covered in blood. Beside him lay a roof tile that had somehow come loose and plummeted to the ground.

Kaley spun around next, almost tumbling as she wobbled on one leg. Harry had to get out of her way to keep from being shoved over, and Matt only just kept hold of her from her other side. When she saw Ross, she screamed in horror.

"We need to call an ambulance," said Lily, both hands against her face like that famous screaming painting.

Emily nodded, reaching into her jacket pocket for her phone. But Harry grabbed her arm and shook his head. "No, you can't! We're all off our heads on pills. If the police come…"

"What are you doing? Ross needs help."

"My dad will literally end me."

Kaley dropped onto the pavement beside Ross and patted his cheek. "Babe! Babe, wake up, please. Come on, wake up. Ross!"

Ross's eyelids fluttered, but he gave no other response. His arms were rigid at his sides.

Lily stood on the kerb, looking like she was about to throw up.

"What the hell happened?" Matt looked around, turning in a circle. He obviously assumed someone had attacked Ross.

"A roof tile," said Emily, barely able to believe it. She lifted her phone with a shaking hand and dialled 999. "I'm calling."

Harry looked like he was going to stop her again, but this time he nodded. "Shit, yeah, of course. Get help. What was I thinking?"

Kaley put her hands on Ross's chest and sobbed. "Tell them to hurry. Tell them!"

Emily made the call. She told them to hurry.

The two seagulls took off into the night, squawking – *haw-haw-haw*.

The ambulance took twelve minutes. Emily knew because she kept checking her watch while they waited. To everyone's relief, Ross had regained consciousness, but only enough to moan miserably as he lay in Kaley's arms. His left eye socket was bulging from the swelling and a horrible gash parted the bridge of his nose where the tile had hit. A freak accident.

A pair of female paramedics arrived and fitted a neck brace to Ross and secured him to a stretcher. Then they lifted him into the back of the ambulance. They'd also washed Kaley's foot and applied a gauze, but they seemed in no rush to help her further. In fact, neither woman seemed approving of the state they were all in. Emily had tried her best to sound sober, but she knew she had failed the oral exam.

"You lot need to get home to bed." The woman's name badge read: Bernie. "The only thing you'll find at this time of night is trouble."

Emily nodded. "I know. We're sorry. Is… Is Ross going to be okay?"

She shook her head and sighed. "His nose is broken and he most likely has concussion. With a little luck he'll be okay."

Luck, thought Emily. *That's something we've had none of tonight.*

He walked underneath a ladder.

"You won't be able to see him tonight," said the paramedic, shoving Ross the last few inches into the back of the ambulance. He let out a moan as she slammed the doors. "So go home and get some water down you."

"We will," said Emily. "I promise."

Kaley had remained sitting on the pavement, wiping tears from her eyes, with her bandaged foot propped up on her knee. Emily sat down beside her now, worried she might fall if she didn't take a rest. "You okay?"

"This is the worst fucking night, Ems."

"He's going to be all right. Probably not thrilled, but… okay."

"You don't know that, Ems." She shook her head and a tear spilled down her cheek. "The state of his face…"

Emily shrugged. "Eh, he wasn't that handsome to begin with."

Kaley looked at her in disbelief. Then she let out a choked giggle. "You bitch! You know I like him."

She put a hand on Kaley's knee and smiled. "Then you should tell him. What reason do you have not to?"

"I just don't want to make things weird. What if he freaks out?"

"He won't. Probably the only reason he hasn't thought of you like that is because he assumes he doesn't have a chance. You're gorgeous. Like one of those Bollywood princesses."

She smiled and did a silly little bhangra dance with her hands. Emily had seen Kaley dance plenty of times before and she was fire, even when messing around and being silly. "I can't believe he got hit by a roof tile. It's, like, the most unimpressive story ever. We're going to have to come up with something better."

Emily nodded. "Like… he got hit by a van after diving to save a puppy in the road."

"That's the one. That's what we'll tell people. Especially if I ask him out and he says yes. I'm not having a boyfriend who got knocked out by a roof tile."

Emily chuckled. The ambulance lights flashed silently, casting a glow over the road. It highlighted people standing on the promenade.

The Syrians.

The group of young men stood silently, watching. Dante was at the front, shaking his head sadly. His jumper was no longer around his waist. He was wearing it.

Good luck, he had wished Emily underneath the pier. Since then, they'd had two injuries.

She stood up.

Kaley frowned. "What are you doing?"

Emily stormed across the road, not even knowing why she was angry or what she wanted to say. Dante saw her coming and put up a hand. "Are you okay?" he asked her.

His concern surprised her and caused her to slow down. "Wh-What are you all looking at? You think this is entertaining?"

Dante shook his head. "What has happened?"

"Our friend is hurt. Really bad."

Dante nodded sympathetically, but his companions were unmoved. Each of them sported various bruises on their faces and unsympathetic sneers upon their lips. The one who Matt had hit with the bottle was missing, probably headed to the same place Ross was.

"I'm sorry about your friend," said Dante.

"Did you…" Emily shook her head. It was crazy. *Did you have something to do with this?* "Look, we're all sorry about what happened earlier. We'd been drinking and… we're sorry."

Dante stepped aside and pointy-beard took his place – had he called him Samaan earlier? His right eye was closed with swelling, and his lip was bulging. Unlike before, he no longer seemed enraged. "I accept your apology, woman."

Emily felt a weight remove itself from her chest. "What were you saying earlier beneath the pier? Were you… were you cursing us?"

"It is good that you have apologised," he said, ignoring her question. "Wise."

Emily nodded. "So we're okay now?"

Samaan shook his head. "No. Your friend said many bad things. I would like to hear him apologise also."

"Oh, okay. I… um. I'm not sure right now is the best time for that. Our friend is about to go to the hospital."

"He beat me and said things I will not forget. He wished for my people to drown." Some of his vitriol returned, the recollection stoking his anger. "I am willing to forgive, but it was he who led your actions as a group. It must be he who repents."

"Repents? What are you talking about?" She looked at Dante, but he averted his eyes.

"Hey!" Harry called over from the other side of the road. His concerned expression showed itself every half a second as the flashing ambulance lights lit his face. "What's going on?"

"Nothing," she called back. "I was just saying sorry about earlier."

Harry marched across the road. Matt moved to the edge of the pavement to follow him, but seemed to change his mind and stayed with the girls.

Samaan puffed out his chest and grabbed his beard, yanking it into a devilish point. "Hello again," he said. "I see misfortune has befallen you."

Harry frowned. "My mate got hurt. You think it's funny?"

"Do you see me laughing?" Samaan was far away from

humour. His dark eyes lacked joy of any kind. "One of my friends is also badly hurt, thanks to you and your friends. Perhaps you will see him at the hospital."

Emily reached out and took Harry's arm as he joined them on the promenade. "What happened earlier was our fault. That's what we said, right?"

Harry nodded, but he seemed to grit his teeth as he did so. "Yeah. It shouldn't have happened, mate. It's my bad."

"You are sorry?" asked Samaan. "You are sorry for attacking us without cause?"

"It's done with, innit? Water under the bridge. No harm done."

"And we're sorry," said Emily, urging Harry with a subtle nod.

Harry shrugged. "Yeah, whatever."

Dante sighed. Emily caught his eye and wanted to pull him aside to speak with him. He seemed to be on her side, but she wasn't sure why. There were questions she wanted to ask him, although she wasn't sure which ones.

"I want to hear you say you're sorry," said Samaan, narrowing his non-swollen eye at Harry. "I want to see you offer your hand in peace to me and my brothers. Repent and ask for our forgiveness."

Harry licked at his lips, clearly still a little high from the ecstasy. "Don't push it, Iqbal. I shouldn't have twatted you, fair enough, but that don't mean I want you here."

A crooked smile crossed Samaan's face. "Apologise and shake my hand, or suffer the consequences."

Dante sighed. "Let us all embrace peace, yes? We mean no harm and only wish to know the same of you."

"Just apologise," said Emily, shaking her head at Harry. "What's the big deal?"

Harry pulled a face at her. "I get that you're upset about earlier, Ems – it was fucked up, I already admitted that – but I believe what I said about this country. It's being invaded."

"This isn't about that. People have been hurt tonight."

"Look, if you want me to apologise, fine, I will, but…" He shrugged. "I dunno, maybe you just don't get it."

"Get what?"

Samaan grunted. "Last chance. Listen to your woman and ask for my forgiveness."

I already apologised for the attack, but it isn't enough. Samaan wants to push things and humiliate Harry. He's not a nice guy.

An engine rumbled to life on the other side of the road. The ambulance was about to leave. Kaley was still sitting on the pavement, sobbing into her hands. Matt and Lily were trying to console her.

Emily sighed. "I'm sorry about earlier, but our friend is hurt, and we don't have time for this. Come on, Harry, let's go."

Harry smirked at Samaan as he took her hand, but she no longer cared if he was sorry. They crossed back over the road together and rejoined their friends.

Emily couldn't help but glance back one last time. She saw Dante shaking his head and staring at the ground. For some reason, he seemed sad.

CHAPTER
FIVE

EMILY'S HEAD WAS BANGING, her mouth dry. With her eyes still closed, she reached out and found a glass of water on her bedside cabinet. But when she put the glass to her mouth, it was empty.

Opening her eyes was an ordeal. They were glued together. "Please… kill me."

Her bedroom door burst open, making her yelp.

"Your boss has been calling," her mum said, moving to the end of her bed. "If I'd known you had work today, I would've woken you up."

Emily bolted upright. She was still wearing her jeans and work shirt. Had she not set her alarm clock? Its digital display was blank, and when she reached over and tapped the buttons on top of it, nothing happened. "What time is it?"

"Just gone eleven." Her mum reached out to her with something in her hand. "I made you a cuppa. You must have got home late last night because I didn't hear you come in. Hope it was worth it, sweetheart." She meant no offence and made it clear with a lighthearted chuckle. "I told your boss you were unwell during the night and that you would drag yourself in as soon as you could. Play along and you might get away with it."

Emily took the mug of tea from her and swigged at it thirstily. It burned the roof of her mouth, but her need was too great to stop herself. When she finally removed it from her lips, the liquid was two-thirds gone. With a gasp, she thanked her mum, and then she groaned. "I overdid it last night. I can barely even remember most of it."

"It's not like you make a habit of it, sweetheart, so don't feel guilty. You're only young once." She shook her head and smiled, the corners of her eyes creasing. "I can tell you some stories, and they rarely end with me waking up in my own bed."

"Mum!"

She crinkled her nose and gave a cheeky smile. Emily had inherited her blonde hair from her mum, but that was where the physical similarities ended. "Sorry, honey. I'll leave you to wake up. You want some breakfast?"

"No, thanks. Don't you need to get down the post office?"

Her mum frowned. "It's Sunday, dear. When do I ever work on a Sunday?"

"Oh, yeah. God, my head is a mess." She rubbed the fuzziness from her eyes so hard she ended up seeing stars. "Okay… I'm okay. I'll be down in a minute."

Her mum nodded and left the room.

For five minutes, Emily stayed in the warm cocoon of her bed. The last thing she wanted to do was get up and see John, or members of the public, but when her mobile phone vibrated on her dresser, she knew she had to get it over with.

She got up and pulled on a clean work shirt, but kept the same jeans. A spot of blood marred the cuff of one ankle, and it brought everything flooding back. Kaley had cut her foot open. Ross had ended up in the hospital.

Last night was rotten.

We could have ended up in jail.

Before she left her bedroom, she messed with her alarm clock again, curious to know why it hadn't gone off. She tapped at the buttons once more, but it wasn't until she picked the unit up that she realised it wasn't plugged in. "How on earth…?"

The clock had been on her bedside table for years. She never unplugged it – there were plenty of other sockets if she needed them – and her mum would not interfere with her things either. It made no sense. But she was late for work; no time to solve riddles.

She hurried down the stairs, missing the last step and crashing into the wall. She shook it off with a few choice words, and then contemplated grabbing a biscuit to eat. But even that would be too much for her sloshing tummy to endure. Instead, she downed a couple of painkillers that her mum had placed on the breakfast bar along with a tall glass of water. "Thanks, Mum," she shouted into the lounge, where the TV was switched to the True Crime channel. It was playing a repeat episode – the one about the train crash in Ronchurch last year where a young lad and his foster carer were the only survivors. If she recalled correctly, the episode was called *Hell Train*.

"See you when you get home," her mum called back. "Hope you feel better."

"Me too," Emily mumbled. "Me too."

She took the bus to work, but it was twenty minutes late. Then the seat she chose was covered in gum, which meant her butt ended up covered in gum. Next, she nicked her hand on a loose screw jutting out of the window frame. Every mini-disaster made her head throb worse and the urge to scream a little more insistent.

She eventually made it to work, but then paused outside the entrance to *Rube's News*, not wanting to go in. The thought of working for the next several hours made her want to cry. Her body ached and her mind was awash with a vague, meandering anxiety. Eventually, she bit the bullet and went inside.

John was right in her face after two steps. "What the hell, Emmie? You knew I was on my own."

"I know, I know. It was a rough night. I'm not well."

He squinted, like he was trying to peer inside her skull. "What's wrong? You got a tummy bug? Can I rely on you today?"

"Yes! I just didn't sleep very well. I'll be fine."

"You look like hell."

"Gee, thanks."

Katie appeared from behind the biscuit and breakfast shelf and waved a bandaged hand. "Hey, Ems."

Emily frowned. "Huh? I thought you couldn't make it in this morning."

"John called this morning saying he couldn't get hold of you, so I came in to cover."

To cover your own shift? I'm the one who's covering.

John put his hands on his hips and clucked his tongue. "You've inconvenienced us both. Katie should be home resting after her accident."

My night wasn't a rave either.

If she's here, why didn't you leave me to have my day off?

Emily sighed and stepped around John. She couldn't stand there and listen to him – nor even look at him – so she went to take a seat. "How's your hand, Katie?"

"Three stitches, and I lost some feeling in my thumb. Doctor said it will hopefully go back to normal once the swelling goes down."

Emily moved behind the counter and sat down on the swivel chair. "I'm glad you're okay. I'll handle the register."

"Thanks. I had to give change earlier. It was awkward."

"I'll bet. Does it still hurt?"

"Yeah, a bit. Aches, mostly."

John was still standing near the entrance, muttering to himself and shaking his head. "Right!" he suddenly said. "I'll be in the office if anyone needs me. Emily? I need you to stay until half five. I want to give the store a good clean, ready for the week."

"What? John, I'm not even meant to be here today. Don't make me stay late."

"I'm sorry, but it needs doing. I'll be staying, too, so you can't complain."

Yes, I can.

She rolled her eyes, too hungover to argue. "Fine, but I want time back in the week. I need a rest, John."

"I'll see what I can do." He disappeared into the office, where he would probably stay for the rest of the day. She didn't even know what he did most days other than send a few emails and stare at meaningless spreadsheets. One time, she was pretty sure she'd walked in on him about to have a wank.

Where's the cup of coffee you promised to have ready for me, boss? Damn, I'm so sick of this place.

It was unlike Emily to feel so angry, but she was clenching her fists so hard that her nails dug into her palms. She felt sick to her stomach, and all she wanted to do was climb back into bed and not see anyone besides her mum.

She can bring me Super Noodles and hot chocolate, like she did that time I had the flu.

"Sorry you had to come in," said Katie. She was slicing open a long cardboard container with a box cutter. "I told John at the hospital that I would probably be okay to work, but he kept telling me to rest. I think he was trying to impress my mum. Act like a good guy, you know?"

Emily grimaced. "He was flirting with your mum?"

Katie glanced towards the office door and laughed sheepishly. "I think so. Gross, right?"

Everything about that man is gross. "I think he's just lonely."

"Yeah, maybe. He's not even that bad-looking." She reached into the cardboard box and pulled out a pink, flowery child's umbrella. In a hushed voice, she added, "It's just his personality."

"What are those?" Emily raised an eyebrow. "Brollies? Since when do we sell those?"

Katie shrugged. "Came in on the delivery. John said to stick them on an end aisle. There's a stand here in the box for them. I think they're cute." She gripped the U-shaped handle and ran her other hand up the painted metal shaft.

Emily felt a shiver up her spine. "Katie, don't!"

Katie released the umbrella. It popped open to reveal a cute pink canopy. "Aw, unicorns," she said. "You see them?"

Emily realised she had a hand out in front of her and was up out of her seat. She tried to move, but couldn't.

Katie frowned at her. "You okay? What's wrong?"

"It's bad luck to open an umbrella indoors."

"Oh, you believe in that stuff?"

Yes. I don't open umbrellas indoors. I don't put new shoes on the table. And I don't walk under ladders.

Ross.

"I just don't like tempting fate," she said, gripping the edge of the counter. "C-Can you close it, please?"

"Sure." Katie closed the umbrella and placed it back inside the cardboard box. "There's no such thing as bad luck, so don't worry."

Yes, there is such a thing as bad luck.

And last night, my friends and I were cursed with it.

Katie looked at her curiously. "Are you sure you're okay? You look a bit rough."

Emily glanced around the shop, expecting things to fall off the shelves, or for the ceiling to cave in, but nothing happened. "I'm fine," she said. "Just… be careful today, okay? I don't want you getting hurt again."

Or me.

I don't want to get hurt.

. . .

Emily was blessedly feeling better by the time her shift ended. It had been a quiet day, and even though Katie had left at two, she had done so only after having replenished the shelves. To spite John, Emily had been cleaning throughout the day, so when the store closed, it was almost fully spruced. It meant that when half four arrived, he had no choice but to let her go. As usual, he offered to drive her home, but she gleefully told him Harry was waiting to collect her.

She and her friends were going to see Ross. He was at home, resting. His injuries weren't as bad as they'd feared.

Or maybe they are. How bad is concussion? I've never had one.

Lily had been texting throughout the day with updates, and when Ross had been cleared to go home at around two thirty, it had brightened Emily's mood. Suddenly, all of her silly fears about curses and bad luck had gone away. Nothing bad had happened, even after Katie had opened an umbrella indoors. The Syrians had been messing with her and her friends, which was no less than they deserved. They *should* be punished for what they had done.

For what Harry started.

I hope he never behaves like that again.

Emily's reservations went away once she was in Harry's car – an old Peugeot 306 his dad had bought him. It smelled of cigarettes, despite him not being a smoker, and it rattled whenever it went above ten miles an hour, but that didn't distract her from enjoying his company. He seemed genuinely pleased to see her, and he had kissed her cheek when she had got in beside him. "I've been thinking about you," he said once they hit the main road.

"I've been thinking about you too. How are you feeling?"

"Pretty rough, but it was a rough kind of night, huh? I'm just glad Ross is okay. What happened to him was crazy."

"Yeah, it was. A roof tile, of all things."

"Maybe he should think about suing."

"Nah, he's not the type. Ross never blames anyone for anything."

"Yeah, he's pretty decent, huh? Anyway, let's go see him so we can laugh about it."

She buckled in and sat back, closing her eyes to catch a few minutes' rest while they drove. Despite feeling better, she was still badly behind on sleep. She didn't want to look in a mirror for fear of what would stare back at her.

The journey took ten minutes, and when they arrived in front of Ross's driveway, Lily, Kaley, and Matt were already waiting. Matt's car was parked in the driveway next to Ross's dad's BMW.

"Looks like we're late," said Harry, switching off the engine.

Emily got out and gave the girls a hug and Matt a friendly nod.

"You okay, Ems?" Matt asked her.

"Yeah, you?"

"Bit of a sore head, but not as sore as Ross's."

She chided him for his lack of compassion, but she couldn't help but laugh.

Lily knocked on the front door. They all went inside once Ross's mum let them in. She told them Ross was upstairs in bed, and they found him awake and pleased to see them. He waved a hand weakly as they entered, and he smiled at each of them as they perched in various spots around his bedroom. A white bandage covered his head, like Mr Bump, and both his eyes were black and swollen.

His room was spacious and the carpet luxuriously thick, but the decor was a little drab and old-fashioned. Most of the heavy wooden furniture had probably been in his family for generations, unlike the cheap Ikea matching set she had in her own room. She perched on a wooden bedside table and squeezed his shoulder gently. "How's your brain, babes?"

"Concussed."

"Does it hurt?"

He nodded slowly. "It feels like a giant hand is crushing my skull, and I want to throw up constantly. My nose is broken too. Mum doesn't believe what happened. She thinks I got in a fight."

"You did," said Matt. "You had a black eye even before that tile hit you."

Ross put a finger to his lips. "If she finds out, she'll chop me up and make fried rice out of me."

Kaley grimaced. "I knew the food tasted dodgy at your restaurant."

Ross managed a chuckle, although it clearly pained him. His thick black hair stuck out of the bandage at the top, damp with sweat. "Never order number twenty-six from the menu."

"So what's the verdict?" asked Harry. He was sitting on a wooden desk over by the bedroom's single window. "How long you gonna be stuck in bed for, mate?"

"A week maybe. I'm pretty dizzy at the moment. Actually, I could use some help getting to the toilet. I'm bursting."

Kaley was leaning up against the door, taking the weight off her injured foot, but she pushed herself forward now. "I'll help you, babes. Just so long as I don't have to hold it for you."

Ross blushed. "I only need a hand getting down the hallway. I can manage the last part on my own."

Harry grinned. "You sure? Don't want you to pee on yourself, mate."

"I'm certain." Ross threw back the covers gingerly. Emily went to avert her eyes, but he was wearing tracksuit bottoms and a T-shirt. Both were sodden with sweat, but he didn't seem to notice. "Okay," he said. "Give me some space to stand up."

Emily moved away from the bedside cabinet and stood against the wall as Ross swivelled around and got one bare foot on the floor. He reached out to grab Kaley's hand as she stepped forward to help him—

—but as he rose onto one leg, his other tangled in the sheets behind him. He missed Kaley's offered hand and fell sideways.

Kaley yelped and tried to catch him, but she was too late.

Ross made no sound as he fell, but the *clonk* of his head striking the bedside cabinet echoed around the room.

"Shit!" Harry flinched and leapt off the desk. "Fuck!"

Emily dropped to her knees on the fluffy carpet. "Ross? Oh my God!"

A bloody smear marked the sharp corner of the wooden bedside cabinet.

She grabbed Ross and rolled him onto his back, shaking him desperately to see if he was okay.

He wasn't okay.

The bandage covering Ross's head had turned red as blood seeped into the fibres. The side of his skull dipped inwards like a cracked eggshell. His left eye bulged horrifically out of its socket. For a single second, Emily's screams caught in her throat, but then she screeched so loudly that her vocal cords nearly tore. Kaley and Lily joined her.

"Shit!" said Harry in the background. "Shit! Shit! Shit!"

CHAPTER
SIX

EMILY SAT in the hospital's waiting room, unable to speak, unable to even swallow. The sight of Ross's misshapen skull had imprinted itself on her mind and she could see nothing else. Her friends in the room also sat in silence. Disbelief was an understatement.

Ross had gone straight from the ambulance to an operating theatre. His mum had gone with him, completely beside herself, howling hysterically and shaking as if she were about to go into convulsions.

I've never seen someone so hysterical. I'll never forget it.

It had now been ninety minutes since Emily and her friends had arrived at the hospital. They hadn't heard a thing during that time. They weren't family, so the nurses didn't care about them, and Ross's parents were somewhere else in the hospital. Emily had glimpsed Ross's father when he had first arrived. The short, stocky man had seemed ready to strangle someone.

Do Ross's parents blame us?

It was an accident.

Two accidents. He hit his head twice.

"I think we're cursed," she said out loud. The small room

seemed to swallow up her words, but she knew her friends had heard her. They looked at her through half-closed, teary eyes.

"What are you talking about?" asked Kaley.

"Samaan put a curse on us," she said. "We were joking about it before, but I think it's true. Kaley hurt her foot, then Ross got hurt. My alarm didn't go off this morning and my bus was late."

Kaley folded her arms and tutted. "You woke up late, so now you think we're cursed?"

"Hey," said Harry. "Easy, yeah? We're all upset."

Lily huffed at him. "Well, if we're cursed, it's because of *you*."

He frowned. "What do you mean?"

"I mean, you attacked those lads last night, so if one of them cursed us, it's your fault."

"Are you saying Ross is here because of me? Are you fucking crazy?"

Lily looked away. "I'm just saying."

"No one is cursed," said Matt, leaning forward in his chair and propping his chin on his hands. "Get real, will you? This is just... fucking shit! It was a terrible accident, but Ross is gonna pull through."

Emily didn't want to argue, and Harry was clearly angry now that Lily had accused him, so she stayed silent. Lily might have had a point about Harry starting the fight with the Syrians, but he couldn't have known what would happen. If the curse was real, Samaan was the only one to blame.

He only wanted an apology. Why didn't I just make Harry give one?

Because I didn't like him calling me woman. *I decided he was bad.*

She stood up – and almost fell right back down. Her legs were hollow and her stomach empty. "I need to go take a walk. Does... Does anybody want a drink?"

"I could do with a coffee," said Kaley, but everyone else

declined. A water dispenser in the corner had kept them refreshed during the last hour.

Emily exited the small waiting room.

Clinical smells wafted over her – bleach, alcohol, and the stale stench of bodily fluids. Weary-looking staff hurried by in both directions, dodging each other in the wide blue-painted corridor. Patients waited on beds outside of crowded wards that could not take them yet. Ross wasn't the only one having a bad evening. The hospital was full of misery – staff and patients both.

I don't know how they do it. Being around so much suffering. Having to manage in such stressful conditions. Maybe working in a shop for minimum wage isn't so bad. If John left, it might actually be enjoyable.

Emily was no expert on the human condition, but she saw haunted, vacant looks on some of the nurse's faces. It was the same expression she assumed soldiers had after combat. She pitied them – good people worn thin.

She recognised one face that passed by her, but it took her a moment to register. Then she jolted in shock and immediately gave chase.

Dante was pushing a mop caddy down the hallway, dressed in white, even down to his shoes. "Hey!" she shouted at him. "Hey, stop!"

Dante didn't stop. In fact, he was rushing. *Is he trying to get away from me? Has he been following me?* She shouted again, this time loud enough that several people in the corridor turned around to look at her. When Dante saw her, his eyes went wide. His mouth fell open.

Emily marched right up to him, resisting the urge to point in his face. "Are you following me?"

"What? No, I work here."

She realised then that he was wearing a hospital uniform. A porter or a cleaner or something like that. He even had on a name badge: *Dante Al Numan*.

"You work here? Really?"

He frowned, the hint of a smile on his face. "You think I'm in disguise? Fancy dress?" Unlike Samaan, he had only a hint of an accent. He had either learned very good English or had been in the UK for a while.

Emily folded her arms, suddenly aware that people were watching her. "What did your friend say to us last night under the pier? He pointed at us and said things."

Dante clutched the handle of his mop and leaned on it. "Bad things."

"Did he curse us?"

"It's not my place to speak of it. I cannot interfere."

"Interfere with what?"

He shook his head and turned away. "I must get back to work. I wish you no ill."

Emily stood motionless as he walked away from her. Once again, it felt like he had answers to questions she didn't even know how to ask. He couldn't just leave her like this without a clue.

It's not fair. I did nothing to him. I tried to stop the fight.

"Hey!" She went after him—

—and immediately slipped.

It happened in slow motion. For a moment, all she saw was the harsh glare of the ceiling lights rushing by, and then she was crashing onto her back with her left leg folded underneath her. The pain came from all over but then honed in on her ankle. "Ah… Ah, I'm hurt."

People hurried to her aid, but Dante beat them all. He dropped down and helped pull her leg out from underneath her. Her ankle spiked with pain and she knew she had twisted it. It was a recurring injury from when she used to play high school sports. She would be running along with a rugby ball one minute, or getting ready for a long jump, and then *twist*! Her ankle would fold beneath her and she would hit the deck in agony.

"Are you okay?" Dante asked, his brow furrowed with concern.

She clutched her ankle and hissed. "I think I sprained it."

Someone came hurrying over, their shoes tapping loudly on the polished walkway. A man in a black suit. He wore an NHS name badge, but she couldn't make it out from on the floor. "Ma'am? My word, are you all right?"

"I-I'm fine. I just slipped."

The suited man stared at the floor beside her, where a puddle of water reflected the glaring light. "Dante? Why is this floor wet? It's the main corridor, for damned sake!"

"I… I didn't see it, sir."

"Unacceptable! This young lady has been hurt because of your negligence. Ma'am, I can't apologise enough."

She waved a hand. "Don't worry, I'm not going to sue. It was an accident."

"Still, allow me to fetch a wheelchair. Dante, I want to see you later when your shift ends."

"Of course, sir."

"Don't give him a hard time," she said. "It's no one's fault." She clicked her fingers at Dante, prompting him to help her to her feet. He did so carefully, placing a hand on her back until he was sure she was steady. "Honestly," she said, limping on one foot. "It's fine. Just a bit of bad luck." She eyed Dante and saw an anxious grimace on his face. "Right?"

He nodded. "Right."

The man in the suit – she could see now that his name was Bryan Coady – gave her a thin-lipped smile. "You're a very forgiving young lady. I'm so sorry a lack of care has caused you to have an accident in the hospital. Rest assured, it'll be addressed and—"

"Are you okay?" Dante asked her.

She nodded. "I'll live. Just need to get some ice on it."

"I'll go get you some."

Mr Coady hissed. "You will do no such thing, Dante. You

will continue with your duties while I take care of this. If you're lucky, you might get to keep your job."

"Stop it!" Emily shook her head in exasperation. "It was an accident and I'm fine. Stop giving him a hard time."

"Ma'am, I don't think you understand. I took a chance with this young man. Most would not have given him the job in the first place."

"Because he's Syrian?"

"What? No! Because he has no experience. I took a risk in hiring him."

Dante grunted. "I'm a cleaner. What experience do I need?"

Mr Coady glared at him but seemed reluctant to admonish him now that she had made her distaste clear. "We will speak about this later."

Dante shoved the mop bucket towards him. "Don't bother. I'll do you a favour and quit. I appreciated the opportunity, Mr Coady."

"What? Now come on, there's no need for that."

Dante took Emily by the arm and helped her to walk. "Fancy a piece of cake?"

She frowned. "Cake? Um, yeah, okay, I guess."

"Good." He led her away as his boss stood in the corridor behind him, calling after him and trying to convince him to stay. For some reason, she felt like Dante had just quit his job because of her. Maybe now he would finally give her some answers.

My ankle hurts.

They sat in the cafe at the front of the hospital. The staff behind the counter were a mixture of old ladies, old men, and two pretty young Polish women. They all seemed to know Dante and were happy to see him. She also noticed they didn't charge him for the chocolate cake or the two coffees.

"You seem popular," she said as they took a seat around a small round table.

"With some, yes. With others, no. The doctors are not friendly around here, but I think they are treated poorly."

"You worry about the doctors? What about the poor nurses?"

"They are the hardest workers of all, but they have, um, what is the word? *Camaraderie*? The doctors, they seem lonely. I don't envy them."

She frowned. "You wouldn't be a doctor if you could?"

"I would like to do work with my hands. My father was a carpenter. He would have taught me if he had lived."

"I'm sorry. My dad's gone too. He moved abroad when I was little, so it's not the same, but—"

He shrugged. "Absence hurts, no matter the cause." He pushed the cake towards her. "Please, enjoy. I got it for you."

She smiled awkwardly. He had such a strange manner about him. He could not have been much older than she was, but it felt as though he'd lived twice as long and seen much more. Perhaps it was the obvious differences between them. He had come here from another country and was trying to support himself, while she hadn't even got a job until she was nineteen, and her mum still washed her clothes.

But that's not my fault. Everyone has problems.

"My friend Ross is really badly hurt. He hit his head last night, and then again today. It was... it was *unlucky*."

Dante nodded. "If I talk to you about this, I invite misfortune upon myself."

She picked up a fork and plunged it into the soft brown cake. "You won't help me, then?"

"I will. To not help you would be wrong, and I fear Allah's judgement more than I fear..." He stopped and let out a sigh.

"What? Fear what?"

He sat back in his chair and exhaled slowly as he looked at her. His eyes were the same rich brown colour as the cake in front of her, but his lashes were much darker. He was handsome in a way she wouldn't usually have considered. Not exotic, exactly, but… striking. He had the same flawless skin Kaley did, but a shade lighter.

He sat forward now and sipped his hot coffee. When he placed the mug carefully back down in front of him, he cleared his throat. "Thank you for defending me earlier, to my boss."

"He seems like a dick. I work for someone similar."

Dante chewed his lip for a moment, staring at his hands and rubbing them together. "He's not as bad as you think, Mr Coady. It's true he gave me a chance when others wouldn't. I think he is just having a bad day, or maybe he has been waiting for me to disappoint him. The people in this country, they treat me like I am an enemy. But I am no one's enemy."

"I'm sorry for what we did. You didn't deserve it."

"You did nothing. It was your boyfriend."

"Harry's not my…" She swallowed and started again as she realised the truth. "You're right. Harry started the fight. I don't know what his problem was, but he's sorry about it."

He raised an eyebrow at her. "Is he?"

She honestly didn't know. "I think so. Look, a lot of people in Boole have mixed emotions about migrants. The country is struggling because there are too many people and…"

He nodded and looked away. Her words seemed to disappoint him. "And you need someone to blame. I understand this more than you know, but it is a poor way to live. By fighting each other, we only weaken ourselves. Take you, for example. Samaan blames you along with your friends for what happened, even though you are innocent – a good person condemned for the actions of those around her."

"I get it. Racism is bad, and we should judge people as individuals, not as groups. I have no problem with anyone who just wants a better life, and in a perfect world we would all live in harmony, but it's more complicated than that, isn't it?"

"Yes, I suppose it is."

Emily's knee was bouncing under the table. Her ankle was swelling in her trainer and starting to throb. The pain was unimportant right now though. "What did Samaan say to me and my friends, Dante? Did he have something to do with Ross's accident?"

"Samaan is not a good man. He is a brother, but one who I fear."

"Why do you fear him? And when you say brother…"

"I mean a brother of Damascus and of Allah, but Allah frowns upon Samaan. In fact, many in my homeland consider men like him to be heretics."

Emily wasn't well versed in religion. It didn't exist within her household, nor in her daily thoughts. "A heretic is what? Someone who believes in Satan or something?"

Dante flinched. "Satan is real – and so are his demons. Samaan worships one of those demons."

"He's a devil worshipper?" She couldn't help but frown, but then she considered what had happened to Ross and decided not to dismiss it so blithely.

Dante laced his fingers together and warmed his hands around his coffee mug. For a moment, he stared at the steaming brown liquid as though it were revealing secrets to him. "Back home, Samaan belonged to a secretive organisation whose members are feared and hated by the common people. The members of this organisation worship at the altar of Klanek."

"Klanek?" Emily's hands were trembling in her lap, so she grabbed them to keep them still. "Who the hell is Klanek?"

Dante sipped his coffee and seemed to doubt whether he should continue. He closed his eyes for a moment before continuing. "The demon prince of fortune."

She tutted. "I get it. He makes people rich if they worship him, right?"

"Not quite. Klanek is responsible for luck – something that defies Allah's plan. His role in the universe is to balance fortune and calamity. Those who worship him are blessed with positive happenstance, while those he condemns are—"

"Cursed with bad luck?"

"Yes. Samaan left the Sect of Klanek when he fled the war in Syria, but your boyfriend's actions angered him into reaffirming his oaths."

Emily didn't speak for a moment. She ate several mouthfuls of cake, enjoying the cloying tang against the sides of her tongue. What she wanted to do was laugh, but she couldn't even manage a smile. Nothing about Dante suggested he was messing around. He believed what he was telling her. In fact, his voice possessed an anxious tone. It scared him to speak of these things.

She needed to ask him what to do. If he understood what was happening, maybe he knew how to stop anything else bad from happening. She opened her mouth to speak, but someone else's voice sounded.

"What the hell are you doing here?"

Harry came racing down the corridor with Matt, Kaley, and Lily a few steps behind him. All four had clearly been crying, but now Harry was angry. "Get the fuck away from her," he yelled at Dante.

Dante stood and put his hands up. "There's no need for temper."

"Like hell there ain't." Harry squared up to him, his teeth flashing in a sneer. "Get away from her."

Emily stood up and grabbed Harry by his arm. "He isn't doing anything wrong."

"Why are you sitting here together?" Harry looked at the half-eaten cake and then at Emily. "What is he doing here with you?"

"I used to work here," said Dante, and then he saw something beyond Harry that made him groan.

Mr Coady was rushing through the cafe. "Dante? What on earth have you done now?"

Harry turned to meet the man. "He's bothering my girlfriend."

"Dante? You resigned your position at the hospital. I must

insist you vacate the building immediately." He turned to Harry and grimaced. "I'm very sorry about this, sir. He was just let go."

"Good," said Harry. "He's a scumbag."

Emily shoved him. "Harry, shut the hell up."

"What is your problem, Ems?" He shook his head at her like she was mad. "Why are you sticking up for him?"

"Because we were just talking, and you're acting like a twat."

Mr Coady pointed to the corridor. "Leave, Dante. Before I call security."

Dante looked at Emily and sighed. "I hope what I told you helps, but it is all I can do." He turned and walked away. Emily called after him, but he didn't stop and soon disappeared around a corner.

Emily slumped back against the table and put her head in her hands. *He gave me answers, but I'm more confused than ever.*

I was right. We've been cursed.

She turned to her friends. "How's Ross?"

CHAPTER SEVEN

KALEY COLLAPSED FORWARD and sobbed into Emily's chest. "He's dead, Ems. He's gone."

"W-What?" Emily looked over Kaley's shoulder at the others and tried to talk around the lump in her throat. "He can't be. No."

Matt's face was flushed. His words came out weakly. "He had a brain haemorrhage or something. There was nothing anybody could do."

"How? How do you know that?"

"A nurse came by to tell us," said Lily. "He's been dead for over an hour. We didn't even know."

Emily's knees deserted her, and with Kaley leaning on her, she couldn't hold herself up, so she flopped backwards onto the chair she'd been sitting in. Her elbow knocked the remains of her cake onto the floor. Mr Coady was still standing nearby, and he tutted as the plastic plate clattered on the tiles.

Kaley fell onto Emily's lap and continued crying into her shoulder. It was a strange situation, cradling her adult friend like a baby, but Emily held her and rocked her as best she could. "He can't be dead," she said. "Not Ross."

Harry sat down on the other chair at the table. "We came

right to get you as soon as we heard, but..." He scratched at his head and seemed momentarily lost for words. "What were you doing with that Syrian?"

"His name's Dante. I ran into him in the corridor. He is – *was* – a cleaner here."

Harry stared at the floor, at the fallen plate. "And what? You decided to have a nice bit of cake together?"

"I wanted to talk to him about last night." She shook her head, not knowing if she wanted to share what she'd learned or to keep it to herself. "I was right, Harry. Dante told me Samaan did put a curse on us. He cursed us with bad luck. That's what happened to Ross."

Lily groaned. "Seriously, Ems. Don't!"

"Don't what? How else can you explain it? Ever since last night we've had nothing but—"

"Babe! Ross is dead because he hit his head getting out of bed. Don't make things worse by telling fairy tales."

Emily grunted. "I'm not. It's what Dante told me."

Harry hit his fist on the table, making her jump. "Dante's a piece of shit who should go back to living in the desert. This is England, not some backwards village in Baghdad."

She shook her head at him. "What is your problem, Harry? Seriously?"

"What's *my* problem? What's *your* problem, Ems? You've been taken in by a bunch of mumbo jumbo, and you're freaking the rest of us out, going on about bad luck and curses. Well, I haven't had any accidents. Why would Ross get hurt and not me?"

"I... don't know. But you have to admit something's wrong."

Kaley pushed up from Emily's lap and staggered backwards, tears in her eyes and snot all over her face. "Yes, something's wrong. Ross is dead!"

Lily folded her arms and looked away.

Matt was shaking his head.

Emily realised her friends were angry with her. They didn't believe what she was saying, and she was hurting them by saying it. "I'm sorry," she said. "I'll stop. It's just that…"

Matt elbowed Lily and nodded towards the corridor. There was a weeping woman walking along, helped by her husband.

Ross's parents. God, they must be so broken.

Emily stood up without thinking. As if being lifted by invisible strings, she floated into the corridor and blocked their path. "Mrs Lee," she said. "I… I'm so sorry."

Mrs Lee lifted her head to look at Emily. Mucus gleamed all over her face and tears streamed from her sore red eyes. Beside her, Mr Lee was expressionless, dreaming with his eyes open. "M-Move out of my way," the grieving woman told her.

"I just wanted to say how sorry I am. Ross meant the world to—"

Emily squealed as Mrs Lee slapped her across the face. In a flash, the mother's grief had turned to anger, and it was all directed at Emily. "He was so smitten with you, but you were never any good."

Emily clutched her burning cheek. "What? I don't understand."

"Do you think I'm stupid? You were out drinking and doing drugs last night. If Ross hadn't been with you, he never would've got hurt. You were always trouble. The lot of you. He was such a good boy. You corrupted him."

"No, we…"

"Move out of my way." Mrs Lee shoved Emily aside, and before she could react, or even say anything, Mr Lee shot her a withering stare that communicated something very clearly.

They wish I was dead instead of Ross. They wish I was gone and him still here.

Emily stood in silence as Ross's parents staggered down the corridor, holding on to each other like they were drowning. No doubt they were headed to get some air and contemplate life without a son. As much as their blame offended

Emily, she could feel nothing but crippling sympathy for them. In fact, part of her wished she was the one who was dead too.

Her friends were staring at her, clearly stunned by what had just occurred. Mrs Lee had known them all a long time. She had always been such a polite and welcoming woman.

"Are you okay?" Lily asked her.

Emily nodded, but then she changed her mind and shook her head. The tears came quickly.

They took a side exit from the hospital, wanting to avoid Mr and Mrs Lee if they were outside. Harry and Matt had both followed the ambulance in their cars and parked nearby. The sunlight was dying out, but the evening was still warm.

Harry reached out and took Emily's hand as they walked. For some reason, it caused Lily to frown, almost like it upset her.

I'm not sure if it upsets me as well.

Do I even like Harry? I thought I did. But now…

He looked at her as they walked, piercing her with those light blue eyes. "I'm sorry about earlier," he said. "It was just a shock to see you with that Syrian lad. Maybe I was jealous, I dunno. But if you say he isn't the enemy, then okay."

"He's not. Whether or not it's true, he *believed* what he was telling me. Samaan is a part of some devil-worshipping cult or something. Dante's afraid of him."

"Well, I'm not afraid of him, Ems, and I don't want you getting scared because of some spooky story. Nothing's going to hurt you. I won't allow it."

His confidence reassured her enough to make her smile. All she wanted was to feel normal again, but she knew it would take a long while.

I can't believe Ross is dead. Mrs Lee was right. He was sweet and kind and gentle. A good boy. Now he's gone. Forever.

"For fuck's sake." Kaley yelled furiously as they headed along the pavement towards the car park. "For fuck's sake!"

Emily turned in a panic. "What is it?"

Kaley scuffed her trainer against the grass at the edge of the pavement. "I stepped in dog shit."

"You really need to watch where you're walking," said Matt. "Isn't that the same foot you injured?"

"Yeah." She kicked at the grass until a divot came loose and she replaced the dog shit with soil stains. "I want to fucking die."

"Don't say that," said Emily. "Please."

Kaley put a hand to her face and moaned. "I loved him, Ems. I loved him and he's gone. If there's some stupid curse on us, I hope it takes me next."

"There's no curse," said Harry. "Chill out."

"Don't tell me to chill out." She turned and glared, pointing a finger at him. "You've only known Ross a few months. The rest of us have known him since we were kids."

"I know that! I wasn't trying to…" He nodded and backed off. "Yeah, I'm sorry. I just want you to be okay and not freak out."

Lily sighed. She went over to Kaley and hugged her. "She knows that, Harry. It's just a lot to deal with. Look, let's just get out of here. I plan on getting drunk for about the next six weeks."

Emily nodded. "I want to go home and see my mum. I… I need a hug."

Lily reached out and gathered her into a huddle with Kaley, wrapping an arm around her and kissing her on the neck. Her nose stud was cold against her jugular. "I got you, babe. Always."

"I know that." As they hugged, Emily spotted a cat emerge from some nearby bushes. It trotted over the road and slunk beneath a parked taxi. A moment later, Harry and Matt led them in the same direction, but by then it was gone.

What is a cat doing at a hospital?

The modest car park was choc-a-block with vehicles, and there was a small crowd of people gathered towards the back. About a dozen appeared to be milling around a specific car.

"What's this?" asked Harry, and when he got closer he became visibly alarmed. "No way. That's mine."

Harry let go of Emily's hand and took off. He'd parked his Peugeot right at the rear edge of the car park, next to a grassy common. It was in a sorry state. An ancient oak tree hanging over it had shed one of its branches. The thick limb had landed right on the bonnet, shattering the windscreen and denting the bodywork.

Emily and her friends joined the crowd. Lily linked arms with her, shivering despite the mild temperature. The assembled strangers were shaking their heads at the damage and whistling. When they realised Harry was the owner, they offered their sympathies. One man said, "That's some real bad luck there, mate."

Upon mention of the word *luck*, Harry glanced back at Emily, but she couldn't hold his stare. She was too busy eyeing the black cat sitting next to the old oak tree. It'd been near them last night, too, when the tile had fallen on Ross's head. It was the same cat; she knew it.

How crazy does a coincidence have to be before it's not a coincidence?

Harry put his hands to his head and swore at the sky. "My old man is gonna kill me. I only have third-party insurance."

Matt patted him on the back. "It's not as bad as it looks, mate. We'll get it into the garage and fix it ourselves."

"Yeah." He looked close to tears, but the words seemed to console him. "Yeah, it ain't that bad, right?"

"Nah, mate. It's nothing to worry about."

Emily stared at the smashed-up bonnet and disagreed. *Things were just as bad as they seemed.*

CHAPTER
EIGHT

HARRY HAD to stay and wait for a recovery vehicle to take his Peugeot away, so he told the others to go. They found Matt's car and climbed inside – only to find it had a flat battery. Not wanting to deal with the headache then and there, they decided to catch an evening bus home. Matt would come back in the morning with his dad.

The eight fifteen bus was late.

Then, after five minutes, it punctured a tyre and had to stop. They decided to walk from there, and Kaley stepped in dog shit again. Matt fell over twice. By the time they made it to Emily's house, they had resigned themselves to something obvious. They were indeed cursed.

Harry met them half an hour later via taxi and they all went to sit in Emily's room. For a while, they sat in silence, just staring into space. While Emily had accepted things already, it was obviously difficult for her friends to let go of their disbelief. To accept that something so absurd could be true… Normal life had been turned upside down, and they were all suddenly afraid of…

What? The boogeyman? A demon? The Grim Reaper himself?
What is it that causes accidents to happen?

Emily's mum brought them all crisps and chicken sandwiches, which perked everyone up a little. No one had eaten all day, and it was now nine o'clock at night. It would still be light out for another hour, but it felt oppressively dark inside Emily's room. She switched on the main light and both bedside lamps, but it remained gloomy.

Matt took a bite of his sandwich and swallowed. He then made eye contact with Emily, breaking the unspoken truce of the last ten minutes, where they had all been sitting in silence. "What did that Syrian lad say to you?"

"Dante?" Emily shrugged, wishing she didn't have to go through it all again. "He told me Samaan was part of some devil cult in Syria that worshipped a demon in charge of luck – or bad luck. It all sounded crazy, but the way he told it…"

Lily was sitting on the bed beside her with a hand on her thigh. It was comforting, but she had left it there a little too long. "We believe you, Ems. Tell us what he said."

"That was pretty much it," she admitted. "Harry came and chased him away before he finished."

Harry sighed. He hadn't touched his sandwich, and the plate sat on his lap. "I acted like a dickhead. Again."

Emily nodded, glad to hear him admit it. Dante had had more to say, if only he'd been allowed to continue speaking. "I have no idea how to reverse things," she said. "Or if we're all going to end up like…" She let her head drop.

"Like Ross," said Matt.

"He was a good person," said Kaley. She'd calmed down a little since leaving the hospital, but it looked like she'd wrestled a bear. Exhaustion bled from every pore, and her coffee-coloured skin had turned ashen. "He didn't deserve to die. I wish I could bring him back. I wish I had fucking superpowers so I could bring him back."

"It's my fault," said Harry, and when everyone looked at him, he nodded to confirm that they had heard him right. "I'm not saying I believe we're cursed, but if we *are*, then it's all my fault. Lily was right earlier. I'm sorry."

Matt screwed his face up. "Screw that. If those Syrian dickheads are putting curses on people who rightfully live here, then they can go to hell."

"Can we stop with the *us and them*, please?" said Emily. "That's what caused this mess in the first place. Maybe if we can find Samaan we can apologise and put a stop to this."

"No way," said Kaley. "If Ross is dead because of him, I would rather slit his throat."

Emily sighed. "You would never kill anyone, Kay."

"Try me. Some people don't deserve to live. Matt's right. Screw 'em."

Harry sighed loudly. "No. Ems is right. We need to keep a level head. If we can't find Samaan, maybe Dante will help us."

"He might," said Emily, "but he lost his job at the hospital. How would we even find him?"

"We could go to the pier," said Matt. "Maybe him and his mates hang out there every night."

Lily took her hand from Emily's leg and hugged herself. "I don't want to go out. What if something happens? What if we get run over by a bus?"

"We could search him up online," said Matt. "Maybe he's on social media."

It was a good idea, so Emily nodded. "Lily, look on your phone. His name is Dante... Dante... Damn, I forgot his surname."

"Well, there can't be that many Dantes in Boole, can there?" said Harry.

Lily got on her phone and tapped away for a few minutes. Eventually, she looked up at them and shrugged. "Nothing's coming up. Any other ideas?"

Everyone was silent. Then a word popped into Emily's head. "Klanek."

Lily's hand hovered over her phone, but she didn't type anything. "Huh? Kleenex?"

"No, Klan-ek. That's the name of the demon Samaan prays to, or whatever. I just remembered it. Look it up."

"Okay." Lily tapped it into her phone. A short moment later, she groaned. "We have a hit. It says that Klanek is a fallen angel and a spirit of the wind. One of Lucifer's knights of hell, who rewards those who serve him with good luck and fortune. It doesn't say anything about curses. In fact, that's all it says."

"Try another page," said Matt. "Is there anything else?"

"Sure, hold on." She tapped away again. "Okay, I have something here. It's a forum on some geeky gaming site. One of those tabletop gaming things, you know? Painted miniatures and stuff."

"How is that helpful?" Kaley complained.

"I dunno, let me look." She started to read. Her expression grew more and more dour. Eventually, she shook her head and passed the phone to Emily. "This is insane."

Emily read the site's message board and read it aloud for the others.

– Painting an idol to worship Klanek. Anybody help?

– Hey. I am disciple of Klanek. What do you need to know?

– What does he look like? I can't find any images of him.

– His image is obscured from men, but he is often portrayed in animal form. A fox or sometimes cat. He watches unseen, manipulating men's destinies. Fall beneath his eye and you suffer bad fate until you die.

– Okay, thanks. Heard you can curse an enemy by worshipping Klanek? Is that right?

– Yes. Klanek can punish enemies, but is not to be messed with. In sixties, Iranian farmer cursed entire village after rape of daughter. Over one hundred people died in space of forty-eight hours. Each met fate via accident. Evil cannot be stopped once in motion.

– That's so cool!!! I have a few people I would like to set Klanek on ;-)

– You are fool. Put blasphemous thoughts out of mind.
– Fuck you, raghead.
– Allah sees our hearts. Pray you meet him free of sin.
– I'll go see him after I finish banging your mum.

Emily looked up at her friends, who sat motionless around her room, not even blinking. "A moderator ends the thread then," she explained. "That's all it says."

Matt chuckled. "Sounds like a fun group. Maybe I'll join up and paint my own miniature bad luck demon. What the hell, guys? Are we really going with this? I'm still struggling to accept that we're all cursed. It's nuts."

Emily handed Lily back her phone, then tucked some loose hair strands behind her ears. Her eyes were fuzzy and tired, but she couldn't contemplate sleeping. "The wiki page Lily just read and those weirdos on the forum all say exactly the same thing as what Dante told me – that Klanek is a demon who's going to kill us. Unless we do something to stop him."

"Like what?" asked Lily. She was fiddling with her silver rings, rotating them around her fingers. "How do we get a demon to back off?"

"We find—"

There was a sudden crash as a picture fell off Emily's wall. It was a canvass painting of a pug she had bought at a car boot. Now, the stubby-faced dog stared up at them from the carpet.

Emily cleared her throat and tried again. "We find Samaan and ask him how to stop this."

"In whatever way we need to," said Kaley, examining her palm in front of her, like Macbeth seeing blood. "I'm done being a victim, and I'm not going to let some random guy do this to us. Time we did something to hit back."

Harry nodded. "I like the sound of that. We can make the bastard call off the curse by breaking his legs if we have to."

Kaley nodded, her face contorted in a way that made her seem like someone else. Someone alien.

"We *talk* to him," said Emily, glaring at Harry. "You don't solve a problem by doing the exact same thing that caused it in the first place. We find Samaan, and we go in peace. Hopefully he's not as evil as the demon he summoned."

Her friends didn't seem convinced, but she had to try it her way.

No more violence. No more death.

Please...

"So we just go to the pier and wait?" Lily seemed unsure. "What if something happens?"

"We just have to be careful," said Harry. "We go slow, watch each other's backs, and—"

Everyone flinched as another picture fell off the wall, this one a multicoloured splotch of paint.

Matt grimaced. "I don't reckon we're any safer hiding out in Emily's room. The roof could fall in on us, or we could choke on your mum's manky chicken sandwiches."

"Hey!" Emily pointed a finger. "Don't be mean about my mum."

"I'm not. Just the chicken she buys. Was it in the reduced section or what?"

Lily made an apologetic face. "He's right, Ems. Sandwiches tasted funky."

Harry still had his plate on his lap. He lifted the top piece of bread and groaned. "Probably because it's gone off. It stinks." He put the plate on Emily's dresser behind him and leaned away like it was infested with the plague. A sickly odour wafted through the room.

Matt put a hand to his mouth. "Great. We're all gonna die of salmonella."

"I feel okay," said Emily. "Let's just hope we can get this sorted before anyone gets ill."

Another picture fell off the wall, this one a portrait of Emily taken in her final year of high school. Her youthful face stared up at them. It felt like a bad omen.

• • •

They didn't bother waiting for a bus after what had happened last time, and they also decided it was too dangerous to call a taxi. Instead, they kept their feet on the ground and strolled carefully along the roadside. They kept to the grassy verges and stopped warily every time a car passed, expecting it to veer towards them or launch a spinning hubcap at their necks. Kaley made doubly sure not to step in any dog shit.

Nothing bad happened.

The lower beach was about a mile and a half from Emily's house. It took them an hour to get there. By the time they arrived, it was late at night, and the pubs were emptying. Taxis zipped back and forth along the main roads, and groups of revellers sang songs as they staggered to the chip shop and pizzeria on the corner of George Road. The stench of greasy food was tempting, but Emily's stomach was too delicate to accept any food after the rotten chicken sandwich. It might have been her imagination, but she felt like she was already growing sick.

The pier was another quarter-mile away, at the edge of the pub district. It had a cafe, a quadrant of trampolines, and a rickety carousel, as well as a small amusement arcade opposite named *Uncle Jack's*. It all closed at seven o'clock, though, so it was unlit and quiet when they got there.

Nobody was hanging out underneath the pier.

"They're not here!" Kaley was limping after the long walk, but she kicked at the sand angrily. "Now what?"

"We wait," said Emily, also limping a little due to her swollen ankle. "They might still turn up."

Matt leant against one of the pier's wooden support beams. The upper deck was held up mostly by steel girders, but there were still several of the original thick timbers that had held the structure aloft since the sixties. "It's late," he said. "They won't be coming now."

"I can't walk all the way back home," said Kaley. "My foot's killing me. I think my trainer's full of blood."

Matt leant against the beam beside her. "We'll rest up a while, maybe get a taxi."

"Yeah." Kaley nodded. "It'll be okay, right?"

A sudden gust of wind came in off the sea. The old pier rattled, bolts and fixtures groaning. Sometimes, when you walked on the deck above, you could feel it sway beneath your feet.

Lily chuckled to herself. "We are so stupid, guys. We walked all the way here and nothing bad happened. There's no curse! No demons after us. Things just got a little crazy and we freaked out, that's all." She put a hand to her head and groaned. "We need to go home and sleep this night off. Ross is gone and we haven't even started to process it."

No one said anything for a moment, not until Kaley bent over and placed her hands on her knees. "She's right. Dante told Emily a story to scare her, and we all got carried away because we were in shock about Ross. We're all grieving. It's messing with our heads."

"I'm done with this," said Matt. "Time to get real."

Emily shook her head. The wind was rippling the inside of her jacket, so she pulled it tight around her. "We have to be careful. What if we're wrong and the curse *is* real?"

"It's not real," said Harry, taking her by the arm and caressing her hand. "I never really believed it in the first place, but now I've had some fresh air and time to think about it, it's ridiculous."

The wind picked up. The pier shuddered overhead.

Seagulls took flight on the beach – *haw-haw-haw*.

"We're not safe," said Emily. "I-I feel it. I feel something dark around us. Don't you?"

"You need to stop now, babes," said Harry, staring into her eyes like a hypnotist trying to make her sleep. "You're going to drive yourself crazy. Look, why don't I stay at yours tonight? Things will seem better in the morning."

He had lost none of his ability to disarm her, so she ended

up nodding – actually feeling a little embarrassed. What if she had freaked everyone out over nothing? If she hadn't tried so hard to convince them, they never would have believed they were cursed in the first place. It was an insane theory.

Just because we read an article about some religious mumbo jumbo doesn't make it true. Klanek is no more real than Satan or Santa Claus.

The wind continued blowing, sweeping in off the distant sea and picking up speed. It sent more gulls flapping irritably into the night sky. Emily watched the white flash of wings as they rose above the pier.

Something's wrong.

"We need to go," she said. "Now."

Harry nodded. "Yeah. Let's go home, babe."

The rattling grew louder overhead.

Emily looked up. The whole pier seemed to shift to and fro. She leapt back against one of the timber supports, her hands clawing at the weathered wood behind her. "Harry, get back!"

He frowned at her, not understanding what was wrong. He moved in front of her and reached a hand over her shoulder, propping himself up against the wooden beam as he leant against her.

Something fell. It glinted in the moonlight, cut silently through the air.

"Harry!"

A large metal rod came down like a spear.

It buried itself in the sand, vibrating in an upright position.

Harry gasped. He turned around and his jaw fell open. The metal spike had missed him by mere centimetres. If he'd taken a single step backwards, it would've impaled him through the top of his head.

"Holy shit!" Matt was pressed up against one of the other beams next to Kaley. His eyes were bulging out of his head. "What the hell just—"

Lily yelped as another metal strut came loose and pierced the sand at her feet. Then another missed her arm by an inch.

"Run!" shouted Emily. "Get onto the beach."

They bolted for safety, threading between the metal support struts and wooden beams, desperate not to bunch up and get impaled. Harry made it out into the open first, turning around and yelling at Emily to hurry.

I am hurrying!

Deadly objects rained down all around her, sending up explosions of sand.

Lily screamed.

Emily made it out onto the open beach. The others were right behind her. The entire pier had shifted, listing to one side. Another strong wind might topple it over completely.

Lily was still screaming. Emily rushed to her aid and realised she was hurt, her face bleeding from a jagged cut on her forehead, the flesh starting to swell obscenely.

"Something hit me," she moaned, blood trickling down the side of her pale face. "It hurts."

Emily grimaced. "Damn it. Hold still."

Lily quivered in pain as Emily reached out and pinched a wooden shard jutting out of her forehead, buried right in the centre of the gash. When she pulled on it, it refused to budge, but then, slowly, it slid out of Lily's forehead.

Emily groaned as she held the bloody one-inch shard in front of her, almost gagging. If not for the bodily carnage she'd already witnessed in the last twenty-four hours she likely would have.

Lily wobbled, so Emily tossed the bloody shard into the wet sand and grabbed her. "You're okay. I've got you."

"It's r-r-real," she said. "We're all g-going to die."

"No, we're not. We're going to figure this out."

"Ems, I'm scared."

"I'm scared too, babes." She looked over Lily's shoulder at Harry and was glad to see he was visibly convinced of what was happening. So was everyone. The terror on their faces said it all.

They were in danger. No more doubting it.

"We're going to figure this out," Emily said, holding Lily tightly in her arms. "There has to be a way."

But what if there's not?

CHAPTER
NINE

"I DON'T WANT TO MOVE," said Matt, standing on an empty patch of beach and peering around nervously. "That metal spike almost made Harry into a kebab."

"We can't just stand around on the beach," said Emily. "The tide will come in eventually, and then what?"

"Nowhere's safe," said Lily. She moved away from Emily and put her hands over her eyes. "Nothing can protect us."

Kaley dropped onto the sand and wrapped her arms around her knees. She stared off at the distant tide. "There's a demon after us. How do you protect yourself against a demon?"

"God?" said Emily with a weary shrug, but then she had an idea. "Hey, I think I know where we can go."

They all looked at her.

The place she was thinking of was only a stone's throw away, so she told her friends to follow her. She led them past the pubs, which were now filled only with staff cleaning up, and then she took them into a street filled with Victorian houses. At the end of that street was St John's Church, a T-shaped building fronted by a large spire and surrounded by a small plot of land. Emily had been christened there as a child.

A sign sat outside the church with bright yellow lettering. It was the first piece of good luck they'd had all night. *Night Church. Weekends. Open till 2AM.*

Harry raised an eyebrow. "This is your big plan?"

"You got a better one?"

"Nope."

"So let's go pray."

They went inside the church's canopied entrance and passed through into a chilly open area lit by several ornate candle stands. Emily expected to see wooden pews, but instead there were two dozen stackable plastic chairs. Only a smattering of people inhabited the church, most sat near the front where yet more candles flickered, and a corkboard covered with photographs hung from a wooden stand. Jesus watched over all from a large stone crucifix set upon the far wall, flanked by two tall stained-glass windows.

Is he real? Can he protect us?

Now they were inside, Emily wasn't sure what to do, so she just stood there, breathing in the muskiness of the old interior.

"Good evening," said a husky voice.

Emily and her friends turned to meet an approaching vicar. The dog-collared man was stocky and bearded, and would've made an excellent rugby player if not employed by God. Despite his imposing frame, he smiled warmly and welcomed them with both arms. "Welcome to St John's," he said. "Is this your first time at night church?"

Emily nodded. "We... We wondered if it's okay for us to come inside for a while?"

"Of course. All are welcome, so long as they respect others."

Matt cleared his throat and gave a small bow. "We promise, vicar."

The vicar chuckled. "You can call me Daniel. We don't do formality here." He motioned to himself and drew attention to the fact he was wearing jeans. "The night church is new," he explained, "so we're still growing at the moment, but take a seat or help yourself to tea." He nodded over to a table with a hot water urn at the back of the room. "Tonight, we're praying for lost souls. People who've been reported as missing. Mitch Chegwin. Sarah Tatlow. Michelle Matthews. Jude Gowdie. We pray for their safe return."

Emily looked over at the photo-covered corkboard. "Does it ever work? Do missing people ever turn up after you pray?"

Daniel's smile faded and the corners of his eyes creased. "Not as much as I would like, but sometimes, yes. The world is growing increasingly dangerous, so it's important that good folk continue to come together and offer comfort to one another. That's why we're open late. There are a lot of night shift workers in Boole. I must admit, it's nice to see some youthful faces here. What brought you to us tonight?"

Emily knew she couldn't come out with the truth. At least not all of it. "We've been having a lot of… bad luck," she said.

Lily pointed to her bloody forehead. "You could say we're cursed."

"Our friend died today," said Kaley. She then shook her head and stared at her muddy trainers. "I'm Sikh. I shouldn't be here."

Daniel reached out and touched the top of her hand as it hung by her side. "Labels don't matter, child. What matters is that we live good lives and trust in a higher power. We all end up in the same place regardless of what we believe, so you are most welcome here. You may worship in whichever way you choose." He chuckled. "Within reason, of course."

Kaley offered a weak smile. "Thank you."

"Take a seat, please."

Emily went to get a cup of tea first. There were few things more calming than a brew, and she definitely needed calming down right now. What happened beneath the pier was crazy. Her heart was still pounding.

Lily joined her at the urn, placing a hand on her lower back and rubbing. "You really think we'll be safe in here, Ems?"

"I don't know, but if a demon is trying to hurt us, surely it can't enter a church. I mean, that's the rules, right? This place is a sanctuary from evil."

"Yeah, vampires and demons and stuff. Like in the movies." She rubbed at her eyes, smudging her mascara and some of the dried blood on her forehead. "I keep expecting to wake up, you know? But every time I pinch myself, nothing happens. I'm being punished."

Emily finished pouring hot water from the urn and looked at her friend. "For what? What did you ever do to anyone, my sweet, gorgeous Lily?"

"I'm not perfect, Ems. I screw up just like anyone else."

Emily took a jug of milk and added some to her tea, along with a heaping of sugar. She then looked up at the high-vaulted ceilings and felt deeply insignificant. "Well, you're in the right place to ask for forgiveness."

"We don't believe in God, Ems. We never have."

She turned and looked over at Jesus, watching them from his stone cross. "Maybe we were wrong."

She took her hot drink over to the rear row of seats and sat down next to Kaley, who still seemed a little awkward about being inside a church. She glanced around uneasily, taking in all the Christianity.

"You think the vicar will let us sleep here?" Matt asked with an anxious titter. "Or live here permanently?"

"I *do* feel safer," said Kaley. "It's weird. This just feels like a safe place, you know?"

Emily nodded. "Maybe it's because the building is so old. The world is so rushed and chaotic, but this place probably hasn't changed in decades. It's insulated from everything that goes on outside."

"We need to find Samaan," said Harry. "Nothing's changed. We find that bastard and make him fix this."

Emily sipped at her hot tea and sighed with pleasure. "But for now, we're going to take a breather."

"Amen," said Lily, and then she blushed. "That wasn't intentional."

"No," said Emily. "Amen is the word. We need a minute to get our heads straight."

She looked at the corkboard again, and while she couldn't make out the photographs very well from the back of the church, she could see that they were mostly young people. How many of them had been killed by demonic curses?

None. Because that would be crazy. They probably ran away or got abducted by psychopaths like Fred West or the Boxcutter Killer. I'm sure a lot more people die due to other people than they do because of minions from hell.

We really are unlucky.

The vicar wandered over to them with a metal tin in his hands, setting it down on an empty chair and opening it. Inside were first aid supplies. "I thought I'd take care of that for you," he said, nodding to the gash on Lily's forehead. "How did you do that?"

"We were underneath the pier," she explained. "Something fell on me. A piece of wood."

"My word! Thank the lord it wasn't worse. Here, hold still."

Lily flinched as Daniel applied a cotton pad and held it in place with a large beige plaster. She thanked him once he was done, but instead of leaving, he sat down.

"You should still get some antiseptic on it," he said. "But at least you look a little less ghastly. And from the looks of all your piercings, you're used to a little pain."

"She's not exactly a good Christian girl," said Harry, and he winked at her.

Lily rolled her eyes. "If Black Sabbath is wrong, then I don't want to be right."

"All hail the prince of darkness Ozzy Osbourne," said Daniel with a boyish grin at odds with his manly beard. When they looked at him, he put his hands together in prayer. "Of all the things for God to concern himself with, I highly doubt rock music is one of them. So, tell me... what has you youngsters looking eighty years old? What's happened?"

Emily shrugged. "Like we said, we're cursed. Do you have any advice for people who are cursed?"

"Cursed? My, you are being dramatic, aren't you?" He scratched at his beard and frowned. "Dear me."

Harry blinked slowly, his eyelids heavy. "You don't believe in curses, then? In bad luck and stuff like that?"

"I never dismiss anything, child. Wise men admit they know nothing. All I would say is that if dark forces such as curses are real, then so too must be good forces, and any foul spirit can be dispelled by one that is pure."

Emily frowned. "Is there a good luck angel we can pray to?"

"Not that I know of, but God watches over all who enter his church, so if you believe you are maligned, try asking for his help. He might just give it."

"Is it that easy?" asked Lily. "We just have to ask and he'll help us?"

Daniel looked over at the stone Jesus at the side of the church. "He's a busy man, but it's kind of his job. If he won't help a bunch of struggling youths, then what good is He?"

Matt pulled a face. "Are you allowed to say that, Vicar? I thought the company line was that God can do no wrong."

"God can't do wrong because he answers to no one but himself, but we are his children, and sometimes children are insolent. Ask God for help. He is here."

Emily nodded. "Thank you, we will."

And so the five of them prayed. Four atheists and a Sikh in a church, asking God to protect them from a demon named Klanek.

Please God, protect me and my friends. We're sorry for what we've done, and we beg for another chance. Please God...

Emily prayed for ten minutes before she ran out of things to ask for. It seemed redundant to keep thinking the same thoughts and making the same prayer. The others stopped around the same time she did.

Matt tapped his fingers rhythmically against his knees and blew air out of his cheeks. "How do we know if it worked?"

"We don't die," said Harry.

Kaley rubbed at her ankle, her head resting against the back of the chair in front of her. When she straightened up, she had a line on her forehead. "We have no way of knowing, do we? We could go outside and get hit by a roof tile like Ross."

"We can't stay here," said Lily. "My dad has sent me like a hundred messages. He's gonna kill me when I get home."

"If you get there in one piece," said Matt grimly.

Emily picked at her nails, thinking things through. "How do we test bad luck?"

"We flip a coin," said Harry.

Matt straightened up in his chair. "You're right. Hold on, let me get one." He shuffled in his jeans pocket and pulled out a handful of change, grabbed a fifty-pence piece, and handed it to Harry.

Harry took the coin between his thumb and forefinger, examining it. "All right, I guess I call heads." He flicked the coin and caught it, then slammed it onto the back of his other hand. "You ready?"

Emily held her breath and nodded.

Slowly, Harry lifted his hand to reveal the coin. The Queen's stoic face met them. "It's heads."

"Do it again," said Matt, his eyes wide.

Harry flipped the coin twice more. It landed heads each time.

Matt was beaming now. "Three heads in a row!"

"It worked," said Kaley, looking up at the statue of Jesus. "Father Daniel was right."

Lily rubbed at the plaster on her head. "So... God is protecting us now? Did he send the demon away?"

"Who knows," said Harry, "but it feels different, right?"

Lily looked around and nodded. "It does. It feels like everything is going to be okay."

Emily wasn't so sure she felt the same way, but it was good to see the relief on her friend's faces. And there was no denying the luckiness of the coin flip.

"It's past midnight," said Kaley. She stretched her arms and yawned. "I really want to go home."

"I think we all do," said Lily. The bruising had crept down to her left eyebrow now, a blueness showing through her make-up.

Harry stood and gave himself a shake. "Let's go grab a taxi then. I'm starving."

Matt nodded. "Me too. Maybe those chicken sandwiches weren't so bad after all, because I feel okay. I'm freezing my nuts off though. It's proper cold in here."

Emily rubbed at her arms. "I know, right? You think they'd have better heating in seventy-year-old stone buildings."

Everyone chuckled. It was like music.

They shuffled out of the row and into the centre aisle. Daniel was standing at the back of the church with his hands on his rotund belly. He smiled at them as they headed for the exit. "Did you find what you were looking for?" he asked.

"I think so," said Emily, giving him a polite nod. "Thank you for helping us."

"My pleasure. It's what I'm here for. Will we be seeing you again?"

Emily shrugged. "I don't know. Maybe."

"Church has definitely grown on me," said Lily, smiling. "I might have to rethink my life."

"Well, you're always welcome here," he said. "Go with God."

"We will," said Matt. "God bless you, Father."

They headed off towards the entrance, passing by the ornate

candleholders. Harry chuckled and mocked Matt in a funny voice. "God bless you, Father."

Matt elbowed him in the ribs. "Shut up. He was a decent bloke."

"Hey, that hurt." Harry shoved him back. "Dickhead!"

Matt's feet came together in a tangle and he tripped, crashing into one of the candleholders and knocking it over. He landed right on top of it.

Father Daniel hissed at the rear of the church. "What on earth?"

Matt muttered words that should not be spoken in a church. But Harry had shoved him harder than necessary. He was understandably angry.

Lily moved to help him, but then stopped and gasped.

Emily smelled burning.

Matt's arm went up like a torch, ignited by the lit candles beneath him. For a moment, he didn't even realise it, but then he broke into a panic. He rolled around on the floor, yelling for help.

Harry stamped on his arm, trying to put out the flames, but it didn't work. Emily took off her jacket to stifle the flames but was shoved aside as Father Daniel came racing to the rescue. The vicar held a thick, intricately detailed blanket in his arms, and he threw it over Matt, wrapping it around his limb and choking off the flames.

Emily staggered backwards, trembling with fright, and she saw the horror gradually take over her friends as the smell of burning flesh filled the air.

Father Daniel put a hand on Matt's forehead and soothed him. "It's okay, son. You're okay." He looked back over his shoulder at Emily. "You kids really are unlucky, aren't you?"

"Yes," she replied. "And there's nothing we can do about it."

CHAPTER TEN

FATHER DANIEL WANTED to call an ambulance, but Matt refused. His forearm was a sticky red mess, and he hissed in agony every time he moved it. But it could've been so much worse.

"At least let me put a bandage on it?" Daniel pleaded.

Matt allowed it, so the vicar got the first aid kit for the second time and patched up his arm. As he worked, Daniel shook his head and muttered to himself. "Did no one ever teach you kids how to behave in a church? That blanket is a hundred years old. Now there's a scorch mark right in the centre of it."

"I'm sorry," said Matt in an emotionless voice. Since the accident, he had been in something of a daze, staring at nothing and barely speaking. His only emotion was that of being in pain.

"You seem like good kids," said Daniel, "so I'll chalk this up to an accident, but you better do some good deeds to make up for it. God will be very angry with you otherwise."

"God doesn't care," said Lily. "We prayed to him and he didn't answer."

Daniel patted Matt on the hand and stood up. His knees clicked loudly and he let out a grunt. "Don't lose faith because of impatience. Miracles happen when you least expect them, not when you demand results after ten minutes of praying. Whatever problems you kids are facing, you won't know their true severity until you're looking back at them from the other side. I have faith that you're all going to be okay. In fact, I'm going to pray for you myself before I close the church tonight."

Emily glanced back and realised that the few occupants of the church were watching them. They had caused a scene.

In a church. I doubt that's done us any favours.

"We're really sorry, Daniel. You're a kind man to be so forgiving."

He tilted his head at her and raised an eyebrow. "If you can't get forgiveness from a priest, where *can* you get it? Now, are you sure I can't call an ambulance?"

"I'll be fine," said Matt. "They can't help me."

Daniel frowned, but he put his hands together and bowed. "Then, for the second time, go with God. Go *carefully* with God."

Emily turned and exited the church. The others shuffled after her. Outside, the wind was whipping along the street and the night had turned cold. She pulled her jacket closed and shivered.

What do we do? Where can we go that's safe?

She needed answers. She needed to find someone who could help her.

Samaan stared at her from across the road.

"What the hell is *he* doing here?" said Harry, and he went to take off after him.

But Emily grabbed his arm. "Don't! We need to stay calm and talk to him."

Harry's fists clenched, but she glared at him until he relaxed. Only then did she limp across the road to meet Samaan. The others followed closely behind her.

"Hi," she said, waving a hand. "How did you know we were here?"

Samaan smiled, but there was no kindness in it. "You are marked. There is no hiding."

"We're not trying to hide. We wanted to find you and say sorry."

"It is too late."

"Why? Why is it too late? What happened last night was wrong and we regret it, but we don't deserve to die."

"No," he said, narrowing his eyes. "You only regret what is happening to you now. Your apology is self-serving, and it comes too late."

"Please…" She reached out to touch him, but he flinched away like she was poisonous. With a sigh, she shook her head. "I never even got involved last night. I was trying to *stop* the fight. Why won't you help me?"

"We pay for the sins of those around us. You will all die." He chuckled unkindly. "But this is good, no? You are so worried about people filling up your pleasant country. Now there will be fewer. In fact, I see one of you is missing already."

"Fuck you," said Kaley. "Go to hell!"

Emily turned back. "Kay, don't. We need to sort this out."

But Kaley ignored her. She pointed a finger at Samaan's face and sneered. "We won't let you get away with this. You're going to pay for what you've done."

He sneered back at her. "But not until long after your dead body has cooled. I will come to your funeral and watch your family weep."

"Okay," said Harry. "I'd say we're done with talking."

Emily tried to stop him, but he barged her out of the way. He reared back and swung his fist, but before he could make contact, his feet went from underneath him and he crumpled to the pavement. Then Matt went to grab Samaan, but he tripped over as well. Both of them ended up on the ground, Harry rubbing at his elbow and Matt wincing as he held a hand against his burnt forearm.

Emily froze in place, her eyes fixed on the dark orbs of Samaan's gaze. "W-What did you do to them?"

"Nothing. They are just unlucky."

"Why won't you stop this?"

He glared at her, but for a split second he appeared to waver. "Because it is time those of the West suffered the consequences of their actions. Your greed and entitlement must be answered. You do not own the world."

Harry got up and immediately launched himself into a tackle. Samaan stepped out of the way and let him go sailing past. He landed in the road, on top of a storm drain that rattled unsteadily. It was a relief when he rolled off of it in safety.

Emily knew she wasn't looking at a demon, just a young man full of anger. She must be able to get through to him. He had to be human. "Please, Samaan, forgive us. I'm begging you. You've proven your point. We attacked you because of the colour of your skin and I'm sorry."

Again, he wavered for a moment, and some of the venom disappeared from his voice when he spoke again. "It is beyond my means now. Your chance to atone has passed. Perhaps you do not deserve what is coming to you, but…" He glared at Harry and Matt. "Others around you are less innocent. Make your peace and die pure. It is all you can hope for now."

He turned to walk away. She reached out to grab him but missed. Matt moved to pursue him, too, but twisted his ankle and fell down.

Emily watched in silence as Samaan faded into the night. The full moon seemed not to reach him. Only the shadows.

"That bastard," said Kaley, her lip quivering. She was trying not to cry. "Why wouldn't he help us?"

Emily closed her eyes. "I don't think he can."

Matt hissed as he tried to put weight on his ankle. "I couldn't grab him. It was like something invisible kept getting in the way."

"We *can't* hurt him," said Harry, sitting on the kerb. "We can't make him change his mind."

"I don't think he has a choice any more," said Emily. She had looked at Samaan's face and seen something. "This has got away from him. He cursed us in anger, then gave us a chance to put an end to it, but we were all too proud to back down."

Harry frowned. "Are you saying we deserve this?"

"No. Just that we could have saved ourselves, but we didn't. And now it's too late."

"This is all your fault," said Matt, turning on Harry. "Every time you drink, you start shit."

Harry rolled his eyes. "I didn't tell you to smash a bottle over someone's head. You seemed more than happy to get into a ruck."

"Only because you got everyone riled up. I wouldn't have gone looking for trouble like you."

"Ah, get lost, you dickhead. This ain't my fault."

"Yes, it is," said Kaley. "I don't know why we even started hanging around with you. You've been a dickhead from the start."

Harry rolled his eyes and tutted. "Are you kidding me? Matt told me you were all cool, but you don't even know how to have a laugh."

"Pack it in," said Emily. "Let's not turn on each other."

"Why not?" said Kaley. "We all know Harry is to blame for this. We were fine until he started hanging around with us. He's a loser and a thug."

Harry was shaking his head and chuckling to himself. "That's just *your* opinion, ain't it?"

"Yeah, and my opinion is that you're an angry, racist dickhead with a tiny cock. None of us likes you."

"Is that right?" He stood up from the kerb and turned around. "Lily, you like me, right? What about my cock? Is it tiny?"

Lily folded her arms and looked away. "I'm not getting involved. This isn't going to help, is it?"

Harry put his hands out in front of him like he was imploring her to answer. "I'm just asking if you like me, Lil. I mean, you certainly seemed to last week."

She turned to face him, her bruised, swollen face giving her a ghoulish appearance as she scowled. "Harry, just shut up, will you? What are you even trying to do?"

He smirked and mimed zipping up his lips.

The subtext was pretty obvious.

Kaley sneered in disgust. "You two slept with each other?"

"What? No!" Lily turned to look at Emily, shaking her head. "Babes, I promise I—"

"Don't lie to me," said Emily, putting her hands on her hips. "Not over this. I don't care if you slept with Harry."

"But... I knew you liked him."

She shrugged. "So what? He's just some lad. You're important to me, not him. I really don't care. It's not that deep."

"I don't even like him, Ems." She groaned, put a hand to her face and shook. "I think I was just trying to prove something to myself."

Emily frowned. "Prove what?"

"That I'm not gay." She put a hand to her mouth like she had blurted it out accidentally.

Emily flinched. Kaley did the same. But then they both pulled faces and shrugged.

"Who cares if you are?" said Kaley.

"Yeah," said Emily. "If you're gay, then be gay. We won't treat you any different."

Lily rubbed at her face, dislodging some of her pale make-up. "I know that, guys. I'm not afraid of losing you, I'm just... confused about me – myself. For a long time I haven't been sure whether I like girls, boys, or whatever, but I thought we'd be closer if we all liked boys and dresses and girly shit. Admitting that I don't..."

Emily hugged her. "You don't have to like boys to be my bestie. It's cool. I love you, Lil."

"I love you too," said Kaley, joining in the hug.

"This is all really hot," said Matt, "but not really important right now, is it?"

"I guess not," said Kaley. "What were we talking about before? Oh yeah, we were talking about how Harry caused all this shit and now we're fucked."

Emily shushed her. "We can figure this out without blaming each other. Kay, this isn't like you. I've never seen you so angry."

"Ross is dead! Do you get that? He's dead because Harry couldn't keep his fists to himself."

"This ain't my fault," said Harry. "We all got into a scrap. None of you cared at the time."

"We were all high," said Kaley. "Because of your fucking drugs."

Harry shook his head in disbelief. "Are you really that much of a hypocrite, you stupid bitch?"

Matt stepped in front of him, got in his face. He was clutching his bandaged arm but seemed ready to fight. "Watch how you talk to her, mate."

"Or else what?" He shoved Matt in the chest, sending him staggering backwards off the kerb. This time he expected it, though, and stayed on his feet. He came to a stop in the middle of the road, fuming.

"I am so done with you." He clenched his fists and gritted his teeth. "Dickhead."

Then the ground disappeared beneath him.

Emily squawked. "Matt!"

"Help!" Matt landed in the road. He'd been standing on top of the storm drain, and the brittle steel had given way. He was now dangling by his underarms inside a hole.

"Oh no!" said Lily, hands over her mouth.

Harry's demeanour changed, and he immediately reached

out a hand to help Matt. Matt took it, but he couldn't pull himself free. "I'm stuck," he cried. "Get me the hell out of here."

"I'm trying, mate!"

There was a flash of light, a vehicle turning the corner and entering the main road. Emily cried out a warning and waved both hands at the driver.

Stop!

The road sweeper was slow, but it was heading right towards them.

The driver was sitting high up inside a cabin, not paying enough attention. As the vehicle got closer, Emily realised he was wearing headphones and tapping away on the steering wheel.

"Stop!" she yelled. "Hey, stop!"

Matt couldn't twist around to see what was coming, but he heard the deep rumble of the engine and the *swish-swish-swish* of the sweepers. "What's happening? What is it?"

Emily raced into the middle of the road, hopping up and down. "Hey! Hey, stop!"

The driver was looking away, barely paying attention. A seagull perched on the top edge of the windshield, flapping its wings. A thick white jet erupted from its backside and smeared the glass. The biggest shit Emily had ever seen a seagull take.

The driver couldn't see a thing now. He obviously noticed the mess, because the windscreen wipers flicked on, but all it did was spread the white-brown slurry around.

"He can't see us," Emily moaned. "He can't see."

"What is it?" Matt demanded, panicking in the hole. Harry tried with all his might to yank him out, but he was completely wedged.

Swish-swish-swish.

The road sweeper was only a few metres away now and still coming. Kaley and Lily screamed at the driver from the pavement, trying to get his attention. The whirring mops forced them to stay back, and the driver's cabin was four feet off the ground. The man was still distracted trying to clean the bird shit off of the windscreen.

Matt begged for help, squealing.

Lily grabbed Kaley. They both turned away.

Harry kept on tugging at Matt right until the last second, but eventually he had no choice but to leap back onto the pavement.

Emily froze in the middle of the road. Her eyes met Matt's, and she knew she would never forget the utter horror on his face – a mental snapshot that would haunt her nights forever. If she had any nights left.

The road sweeper rolled right over Matt, crushing his head and shoulders as they stuck out of the drain. Blood spurted out onto the road, to be mopped up immediately by the sweepers. In the moonlight, gory chunks glistened on the thick fibre mops.

Harry doubled over as something struck him in the stomach. It bounced off onto the pavement with a bloody *splat*! Matt's arm.

"Fuck!" Harry dropped to his knees and retched.

Emily staggered out of the road sweeper's path just as the driver realised something was up. He applied the brakes, but it took several metres for the vehicle to stop, far enough to reveal the empty storm drain behind it – and the scattered entrails of their friend. Matt had been smeared across the road like bird shit on a windscreen.

Everybody screamed.

CHAPTER
ELEVEN

EMILY RAN. It wasn't a conscious choice, more of a primal instinct. The terror put her into flight mode and she took off like a rocket, leaving her shellshocked friends behind her.

Matt is dead. Ross is dead. All the people I care about are dying.
Soon, I'll be next.

She raced along the promenade, knowing she might trip and smash her skull at any moment, but there was no way to get control of herself. Panic had seized her entire nervous system.

I want my mum. How do I get home without… without having an accident?

What if I never see her again?

Her sides were aching, but she continued to sprint, running further than she'd ever gone in one continuous dash. Mortal fear was one hell of a drug.

When she finally faltered into a slow jog – and then a brisk walk – she was back near the pier. It was now well past 1AM, and the pubs were locked up and dark. The taxis were all gone, probably to Boole's only nightclub on the other side of town.

Only a single person inhabited the area, standing in the recess of a doorway, and it caused Emily to stop in fear. It could only be a weirdo, alone at this time of night. It was certainly a man. And he was approaching her.

"Who is that?" she said, hating the frightened quiver to her voice.

"It's me. Are you okay?"

Emily took a step back, and then gasped when she saw who it was. "D-Dante? Are you following me?"

"It was Samaan who I was following, but then I heard about the pier. The police have cordoned the whole thing off in case it collapses. I thought maybe you were..."

"Dead?"

He took a few steps closer. "I thought that maybe there'd been a terrible accident."

"There has been." Now that she'd stopped running, her ribs were beset by stabbing pains. She bent over and heaved in a series of breaths. "Matt's dead. Samaan won't lift the curse."

"He can't lift it," said Dante. He stepped up to her and, cautiously, reached out a hand to touch her arm. "Once a new moon rises, Klanek will not be recalled."

She shook her head, still panting. "What, so there was like a cooling-off period and we missed it?"

"It is just how these things work. A pact is sealed with the passing of day into night."

"Why did Samaan come and find us if not to help? Did he just want to gloat?"

"I believe part of him hoped the curse had failed."

She straightened up and faced him. "I don't want to die, Dante. Please help me. What can I do?"

He shook his head, peering into her eyes. "Nothing. There is only one way to..."

She reached out and grabbed him hard. When she realised what she was doing, she let go and stepped back. "What is it? If there's a way to save my friends, tell me."

"I can't. It would not be right."

Fuck you! She grabbed him again, and this time she didn't let go. "I'll tell you what isn't right. Ross was twenty-two years old and one of the sweetest people you could ever meet. Matt was twenty-three and lost a brother to leukaemia when he was twelve. He spent his teenage years supporting his mum and keeping her from committing suicide. Kaley is studying law so she can fight for people's human rights. Lily once stepped on a toad and killed it, and she cried for three hours afterwards. And me? I was trying to stop the violence last night, and your friend Samaan decided to murder me anyway. That's what isn't right, you bastard."

"Samaan is not my friend."

"So help me! Help me, or you're just as responsible as he is."

He looked down at her hand, which was wrapped around his left wrist. From how hard she was squeezing, it must have hurt him, but he showed no sign of pain. "Some things are not worth the price," he said. "Wouldn't you rather die with a clean soul than live a life with it stained?"

"I deserve the life I was given. You and Samaan have no right to take it away. Murder is a sin, right?"

"Which is why I do not wish to tell you what I know."

She glared at him, but quickly realised he was trying to communicate something to her. "Samaan...? If I kill him the curse will be broken?"

"Black magic feeds off the soul of the witch. Extinguish that soul and the darkness may lose its invite to enter our realm."

She let go of his arm and turned to walk away. "Where do I find him?"

Dante followed, grabbing her and turning her around to face him. "Samaan is a dangerous man. You cannot simply kill him."

"What do I have to lose? I'm dead if I don't try."

"Let me help you."

"Why would you do that? Wouldn't murder stain your precious soul?"

"Perhaps some of us are meant for damnation." He shrugged, looked down at the ground, and then back up at her. His eyes were so brown they almost seemed black. "When I came here tonight," he said, "I thought it was over. I thought you were dead. Instead, I find you here alive. Allah must want me to help you. His light shines upon you, Emily. Your kindness, your beauty…"

She raised an eyebrow. "Are you flirting with me?"

"What? No, of course not. I… You are a good woman, that is all I am saying. Harry does not deserve you."

She nodded. "You're right, he doesn't. He's a prick and I'm done with him."

"He has hurt you?" His dark eyes narrowed.

"No, I just saw him for what he is." She folded her arms and shivered. "You'll really help me?"

"Yes. Are you cold? Here, have my jumper."

She went to argue, but he had already pulled his top off and was wrapping it around her shoulders. He was wearing a long-sleeved black T-shirt underneath. "Thanks," she said as his hands rested on her shoulders. Their eyes met, their faces close. She couldn't say why she did it, but she leant forward and kissed him on the mouth – just a peck.

Dante flinched, and Emily was relieved to see that it was only from surprise and not disgust. He continued to gaze into her eyes, but now he was blushing – and smiling. "What was that for?"

"For being decent. I… I trust you. I don't know why."

He reached out and took both of her hands. "I was not always as you say, but perhaps by helping you I can find my way back into the light."

"Right now, I'm just interested in keeping me and my friends alive. Where can I find Samaan?"

He sighed. "I'll show you."

· · ·

Dante said they could walk to where they were headed, so Emily kept pace with him as they marched away from the town centre. She was warm now that she was wearing his jumper, but she worried about whether it had left him chilly. He didn't complain, though, so she decided it was fine.

The walk gave them time to talk. "Why do you spend time with Samaan if he scares you?"

"Safety. There are only a dozen brothers and sisters from my country in Boole. We stick together to protect one another."

"From people like Harry?"

Dante looked at her and nodded. "We know we are not wanted here. Some of you make that very clear."

"I'm sorry."

He shrugged. "Do not be. There are kind people here too, and many countries would treat us worse. We are housed and fed and given an opportunity to work. You may find it hard to believe, but I love this country. It is my home."

She smiled. "I'm glad you think so. Maybe one day things will be better."

"I fear they will get worse, but that is a trouble for another day."

"Yeah, I guess we should focus on Samaan. What's his deal anyway? Why did he come to this country?"

"Samaan arrived here two years ago to escape the remnants of the war. At first, he sought to rediscover a righteous path and shed his past. All of us knew of his background, but we never spoke of it. It seemed he regretted it."

"So what changed?"

"I don't know. A darkness fell upon him a few weeks ago and he changed. He became quick to anger, lashing out at those around him. Knowing his past, none are brave enough to retaliate."

"In case he curses them?"

"Yes. Most in Syria have forgotten the dark arts, but many

still fear the wrath of those like Samaan. The Sect of Klanek has done many terrible things in its history."

They crossed a dual carriageway and entered a housing estate on the other side. A dried-up stream ran through it and gave off an eggy stench. An abandoned shopping trolley lay on its side, tucked inside a small cement tunnel with a path going over it. Graffiti covered the side of a nearby house.

"Is this Benford Meadows?"

"Yes. You know this place?"

"Only by reputation."

They walked in silence for a moment.

Emily broke the silence. "So… you expected to find me dead at the pier tonight? It was nearly true. The whole thing almost came down on top of us. In fact, I don't really understand why it didn't. Harry almost got impaled by a piece of steel, but it missed him by inches. Why? Why did it miss?"

"I don't know. You must have protected yourself somehow."

She stopped walking for a moment and looked at him. "How would I protect myself?"

"There are good forces as well as bad. Do you carry any charms or things that have brought you good luck in the past?"

"No, nothing like that. I mean, I've always been superstitious, but not so much that I would carry a rabbit's foot or touch wood every time I…"

He frowned at her. "What is it?"

"I was touching the wooden beams beneath the pier when it started to collapse. Harry reached out a hand and leant on it too. I think… I think we were all touching wood when the wind blew in off the sea."

"You were able to ward off the bad luck momentarily. It is fortunate."

"Okay…" She felt a rush of blood to her head. "So I can protect myself by doing things that are lucky?"

"And avoiding those that are bad."

She looked down at the pavement as they walked. It was

made from concrete slabs, but ahead was one with a large crack in it. She hopped over the crack and avoided whatever bad luck it might bring. Then she crossed her fingers and held them up in front of her. "What else is lucky?"

He chuckled at her. "Um, I'm not sure. Spilling coffee? Placing a needle into a broom. Burning sage above a doorway. Many of these things are…" He frowned. "Old fish tales, yes?"

"Old wives' tales?"

"Yes. I don't know if any of them work. You said you touched wood and that it protected you, but in Syria none would think of doing such a thing."

She still had her fingers crossed, and she jumped over another crack in the pavement. Then something happened that she could not believe.

This is insane.

Emily bent down and picked up a twenty-pound note. She held it up to the moonlight, seeing if it was real. For all that she could tell, it was. "That was pretty damn lucky, huh? Here, you take it."

He shook his head. "No. I won't involve myself in another's luck. It's a good sign, yes, but let's not make assumptions. Klanek is a being not to be thwarted."

She deflated. It was true. She was getting carried away.

A demon isn't going to back off just because I have my fingers crossed.

"Is there a chance?" she asked Dante, suddenly weak and tired and emotional. Reality had suddenly slapped her on the butt and told her to get her head on straight. This wasn't a moonlight stroll with a cute boy. They were on their way to go kill someone.

Before he kills me.

Dante reached out and put a hand against her face. "I'll do all that I can to protect you, Emily. This I swear." He leant forward and kissed her, and this time they locked together for several seconds. His lips were cold, and she knew it was because she was wearing his jumper. It only made her kiss him harder and wrap her arms around him to help him stay warm.

He eventually broke away. "Come on, we're nearly there. Samaan lives in the bad part of town."

Emily looked around and frowned. "I thought this *was* the bad part of town."

CHAPTER
TWELVE

"WE ALL LIVE HERE," said Dante. "Not just Syrians, but Polish, Romanian, and Albanian. All the people who you would rather not look at, this is where you can find us."

Emily checked her watch and saw it was now 2AM. Daniel's church would be closing its doors, and nearly all of Boole would be asleep. She worried about her friends and felt terrible for running off on them. Were they okay? For all she knew, Lily and Kaley were dead. She found herself caring very little about Harry.

No, that's not fair. He doesn't deserve to die either. I'm doing this for us all.

Can I really kill someone?

Samaan killed Ross and Matt. If I don't do it, I'll have no friends left. Whatever it takes…

To her astonishment, there were people awake and in the street. A pair of young men sat on a wall sharing a can of beer. When they saw Dante, they nodded hello. Both had shaved heads, but one had a thick scar running right over the top of his skull. He eyed Emily curiously – and then a little lewdly – before finally going back to his conversation. Further along, a woman rocked a baby over her shoulder in a living room with all the lights on. She waved at Dante as he passed by the front of her house.

"You all know each other," she said. "Like at the hospital."

"The people here look out for one another. Not all are good people, but most are."

"That's the same everywhere. Not everyone hates you being here, you know? I… I never much cared."

"But you didn't stick up for us, either."

"You're right. But none of your friends did anything to stop Samaan either, did they? None of us is perfect."

He reached out and squeezed her hand. "But all of us can learn. I would like to know you better once this—"

"Is over?" She smiled. *Am I really going to want to hang around with a guy who's about to help me commit murder? Is Dante going to do it for me? Or does he expect me to?*

I really don't know if I can do it.

There was another group of people ahead, sitting on metal benches at a small park. They were passing around a cigarette and chatting quietly. Again, they nodded and waved as Dante passed.

"A lot of us work odd shifts," he explained. "Some of us evenings, others throughout the night."

"You mean the shit jobs?"

"No job is worthless. We're happy to do it."

Emily realised she was smiling. There was a comforting atmosphere to the area they were in. The same feeling she had whenever she saw distant family during the holidays. Everyone just milling about, chatting, and catching up. "You know, you're lucky in a way," she said. "People aren't like this any more. We keep to ourselves, mistrustful of everyone else."

"Being poor has its benefits. When you have nothing, no one can take from you, so it is easier to trust each other."

"It's nice. I always thought this part of town was dangerous."

"It *is* dangerous. Don't be fooled, Emily. We all stick together here, but these people have no love for strangers. Some are like Samaan, angry and violent. Life has put them here and they blame everyone but themselves. One day, I wish to make a good life for myself, but others here will never change. They are enemies of themselves."

She nodded, and suddenly the people sitting around the park didn't seem quite so friendly. In fact, she noticed their glares as she walked on by. She was safe because of Dante. Without him, these people would not welcome her presence.

I'm their enemy. They think we're all like Harry.

They're judging me like we judged them.

Emily shivered and could only imagine how cold Dante was. "Are we nearly there yet?" she asked. "I want to get out of here."

He squeezed her hand again. "Almost. You're safe."

"Apart from the whole being cursed thing?"

"Apart from that, yes."

"Wonderful." She reached into her pocket and pulled out her phone. Her mum hadn't texted, but she knew that was because she wouldn't want to be a nag. *She must be worried though. I haven't stayed out all night since I was a teenager.* "I'm just going to message my mum, so she knows I'm okay."

He nodded. "Of course. She is a good woman, your mum?"

"Yeah, she is. Raised me on her own. If something happens to me… I just can't think of how much it would hurt her."

"You are alive now, so say the things you need to."

She huffed. "What, in case I die?"

He looked at her.

"Shit, yeah, okay." She tapped out a message.

Staying at Lily's. I love you mum. You're the best. Ems. XXX

It was short and sweet, but it said what it needed to. She just hoped it didn't end up being a goodbye message.

· · ·

"This is it. He should be inside." Dante pointed to a detached house at the end of the street. It was surprisingly large but in a sorry state. Four-foot weeds had overtaken the garden, and a brick wall around the border was crumbling in several places. One of the front windows was boarded up, while the PVC frames around the others were dirty and degrading. There were no lights on inside. Samaan was most likely asleep – or not in.

He was in town not long ago, rubbing it in that we're going to die. What time is it now? God, it's getting on for 3AM. I need to sleep. But first I need to not die.

"What should we do?" she asked. "Can we break in?"

"If we wake Samaan, he will attack us. We should try to be quiet."

"Quietly break in. Got it."

They crept up the overgrown path.

Emily immediately detected a sour smell coming from the drains. It was terrible that anyone lived in a place like this. Wasn't the landlord responsible for maintaining it?

A slim glass pane ran down the left side of the front door. She tried to look through it, but it was frosted, and the hallway beyond was unlit. When she reached out and took the door handle, she found it unlocked. "I can open it," she said. "It's not locked."

Dante put a finger to his lips. "I'll go first. Stay behind me."

Nodding, she stood aside and let Dante go inside first.

She then thought about what she was doing. Could she really trust Dante? He was a part of this, and she really knew nothing about him. Once again, she asked herself if she could kill someone, and finally the answer came to her.

No. I can't kill someone. I won't be able to do it.

I need to beg Samaan. There has to be some way he can remove the curse. I saw humanity in him. He's not a monster.

I'm breaking into his house.

This is insane. What am I doing right now?

She considered running away, but Dante stopped in the

hallway and waited for her. His dark eyes shone and his hand reached out of the gloom towards her. "It's okay."

Emily stepped inside the house. The hallway was cold and smelled of damp. The cheap laminate floorboards had blown, and they flexed beneath her feet as she walked. Dante seemed to know his way around, and he led her confidently to a room on his left.

It might have been called a lounge, for it had a two-seater sofa and a carpet, but everything else about the room was bizarre. Jagged shapes and strange silhouettes occupied the space, unrecognisable until Dante switched on the main light.

"Jesus!" Emily shook her head. "Jesus…"

"No," said Dante, and he let the word hang there.

The room's main focal point was a pedestal against the wall in between two narrow, curtained windows. It had a small skull on top of it, possibly from a cat. Painted above that skull – and in several places around the room – was an X-shape with a circle in the centre. If she had seen it anywhere else, it would have meant little, but in this house – in this *lair* – it was clearly an occult symbol.

"It represents balance," said Dante. He moved to a lamp on a table beside the doorway and switched that on too. "The circle in the centre is Klanek. The cross represents the four primary elements. Water, air, earth, fire."

Emily looked around and spotted more cat skulls and more of the painted symbols. "Samaan is sick. Why would he be into all of this stuff? It can't be power or wealth. I mean, look at this place. This carpet is a hundred years old." She turned to see what Dante's opinion on the matter was, but he had spotted something behind her, placed along the side wall.

She turned her head. "What is it?"

"I don't know." He took a step towards what appeared to be a decorator's table with a large wooden box on top of it. Once near, he ran a hand over the top of it. From the way he wrinkled his nose, it clearly gave off an unpleasant smell. "There's a lid," he said. "Should I open it?"

"You tell me. Everything I know about Samaan, I learned from you."

"I haven't been in this house for many months. It wasn't like this before. Samaan must have changed things recently, after he recommitted to the sect. He has been increasingly secretive. Perhaps what is inside this box will tell us why."

Emily closed her eyes and took a deep breath, then crossed the room to join him at the large box. "Just open it. We've come too far now to be cautious. Maybe we'll find something to help us."

"Maybe it's where Samaan sleeps," said Dante, and he gave her a weak smile. When he saw she wasn't laughing, he turned back to the box. "Okay. Help me get the edge."

Emily grabbed one end of the wooden lid while Dante grabbed the other. After a three count, they lifted. The lid was heavy, held in place by three hinges, but they raised it easily enough. The smell that escaped, however, caused them both to step back, gagging. Fortunately, the lid remained upright, leant against the wall.

Emily didn't want to look inside, but she couldn't help herself. She knew it would be awful. She knew it would be sick.

But she didn't expect it to be a child.

"What the hell, Dante? It's a kid. Did Samaan kill her?"

He shook his head. "I… I don't know."

"God, she can only be twelve or thirteen. Who is she?"

"A stranger to me. I fear she has been dead for some time."

Emily had never seen a dead body before tonight, and it was disturbing how much it still looked like a little girl. She had long brown hair, a tiny nose, and mottled brown skin, lips shrivelled back to reveal creamy-white teeth. Her cheeks were sallow and rotting. A lemon-coloured nightdress covered her body. A soft pillow supported her head. Fresh flower petals had been scattered throughout the coffin, perhaps to combat the smell, but it also seemed like a loving gesture. Whoever the girl was, Samaan had taken care of her in death. Despite that, the corpse gave off a terrible stench and made Emily's gorge rise.

"I-I don't know if I can do this," she said. "I... I can't breathe."

Dante grabbed her and moved her into the centre of the room. There he held her, with the dead-cat altar right behind him. "We can do this, Emily. We will find Samaan."

"I am here," said Samaan, and he entered from the hallway. "What are you doing inside my home?"

Emily recoiled, but Dante held her tight. For a moment, she thought it was a double-cross, but then he moved in front of her protectively. "We've come to put a stop to your wickedness, brother."

All Samaan did was smile. Then he produced a knife.

CHAPTER
THIRTEEN

SAMAAN EYED the both of them from the doorway, but he did not approach. The knife he held was no ordinary kitchen knife. Its blade was so dark that it was almost black. The handle appeared to be carved from bone.

"You don't want to do this," said Emily, staring over Dante's shoulder. "I can tell. Help us, Samaan."

"I already told you…" He shook his head, his bruises shining in the harsh glare of the ceiling's bare lightbulb. "It is too late. Accept your fate with dignity. Prepare yourself for Allah."

She moved past Dante and stepped towards Samaan. "No, I won't. I don't deserve this, Samaan. You're a murderer."

"You and your friends beat me. What was I to do?"

"You could've called the police, but instead you cursed us. If you believe in God, then you know He won't accept what you've done."

Samaan lifted the dark blade and pointed it at her face. "My God is different to yours. He implores the faithful to punish those who trespass against him."

"I've done nothing to you or your God."

"You're a whore. Drinking, doing drugs, having sex with whomever you please. A violation of His will."

"Sounds like it's a violation of petty men, not a forgiving god."

Dante stepped up beside her. "You speak out of turn, brother. Only Allah may judge, and you fail to serve him by worshipping His adversaries."

"Klanek is but a tool, a way to punish the unrighteous."

"He is the unrighteous one, along with all who accept him."

"If a man cuts another man's throat, you do not blame the knife. You ask if the man deserved it."

Emily glanced to the side. This wasn't headed in the right direction. She needed to get through to Samaan. "Who's the girl in that box? Why is she here?"

Samaan flinched. He glanced over at the coffin uncertainly, but he didn't hesitate to answer. "My sister."

Dante gasped. "You never spoke of siblings, brother. I am sorry for your loss, however it came about."

"So am I. Emani was a pure soul. She wanted only to live in safety; something I told her she could find here."

Emily eyed the doorway. There was a chance she could rush past Samaan while he was distracted, but what would that achieve? She would still be cursed. No. Talking was still the best way to end this. "What happened to Emani, Samaan?"

He lowered the knife and sighed. "I promised her a better life here with me, but I could not travel back to Syria myself to get her, so my uncle agreed to bring her to me." He shook his head and looked coldly at Emily. "Their dinghy did not make it. Emani drowned in the Channel."

Emily put a hand to her mouth. Harry had told Samaan he hoped for the women and children of his country to drown, and that was exactly what had happened. No wonder it had sent Samaan into a rage. "I can't understand your loss," she said. "Or your pain. But I have a family too. Do you want to inflict that same pain on them? Ross's parents are devastated because you took away their son. Matt's are going to be broken when they hear how their boy was decapitated and spread across the road like jam. You're spreading misery."

He waved the knife at her and flashed his teeth. "You think I care about their pain? In Syria, Iraq, Afghanistan, children die in their beds because of Western bombs. Those in Palestine bleed in the streets while the world does nothing. Why is death only a tragedy when it happens to rich white Christians?"

"You can't make this right, Samaan. Whatever you say, it's just plain murder."

He averted his gaze, and she thought she recognised shame in his expression. "Perhaps," he muttered, "but it is done now. The bargain was struck. A new moon rose and expelled the day."

"What bargain?" said Dante. He was slowly shifting his weight from side to side, seemingly ready to make a move if necessary. "What did you ask for, brother? What is your boon?"

Someone coughed inside the coffin. A weak, breathless sound.

Emily spun around and gasped. "Oh my God. Is she...?"

"Get away from her!" Samaan lunged at Emily, but Dante leapt in his way. The knife slashed the back of his hand and sent him back a step, hissing in pain. Blood spattered the dirty carpet.

Samaan seemed shocked by what he'd done. He moved back to the doorway, shaking his head in disbelief, but he kept the knife out in front of him. "I-I asked for *her*."

Emily felt sick. The rotten chicken from earlier seemed to float around in her stomach, wanting to come up. Slowly, she stepped over to the coffin.

The little girl appeared dead, her body partially decomposed. Her lips were still peeled back from her gums, but Emily realised now that her body must have been in even worse shape at some point when it was pulled from the Channel, waterlogged and bloated. Klanek was bringing her back slowly –

repairing the damage wrought by death. "She's... She's breathing. I can see her chest moving."

"She is alive," said Samaan, a desperate sadness in his voice. "And soon to be healthy. The life I promised her will be delivered."

Dante said something in Arabic and then put both hands on his head. "You violate the most serious of laws. This is wickedness."

Emily turned and glared at Samaan. "You sold the lives of me and my friends in order to bring back your sister? Is your pain really so unbearable that you would kill five people where others would simply mourn?"

For the first time since meeting him, Samaan displayed clear regret. He couldn't look her in the eye. "I am sorry. My anger led us here, but it is done. I cannot change it."

Emily saw in his eyes that it was true, and she also realised that she could not kill this man. Even if he wasn't much stronger than her, she would still fail to do the deed. She didn't want to die, but she didn't want to be a murderer either. Living with that on her soul would be no life at all.

It's over. I'm dead.

She held herself and sobbed. Dante rushed to her side to hold her. His lips found the top of her head and he kissed her.

"Wait?" Samaan teetered in the doorway as if he were suddenly weak. "Are you two... intimate?"

Emily frowned at him. "What? No! We've only kissed."

"This can't be true." Samaan began shaking his head repeatedly. "No, no, no. Dante, my brother, what have you done?"

Dante eased Emily behind him and faced Samaan down. "What is wrong? Why does this offend you?"

"Because you took away her burden, you fool. Now the mark is upon you."

"What? Are you saying that by kissing Emily, I took away her curse?"

Samaan hissed. "Now it is you who shall die."

For a moment, Emily's mind went blank. It took several seconds to process what was being said. "Wait, I'm not cursed any more?"

Samaan growled. "No. You will now live."

Dante shuddered, took a breath, stood up straight, and smiled at her. "Then it is done. You are safe."

She shook her head and grabbed him. "No, I don't want this. Not if it means you dying instead of me. Kiss me. Give the curse back to me."

"Yes, brother," said Samaan. "Do it."

Emily tried to kiss Dante on the mouth, but he dodged away. "No," he protested. "If Samaan cares nothing for you, then let him live with the burden of killing a brother." He turned to face Samaan, steely eyed and resolute. "You spoke of consequences. Here they are."

"This isn't your fault," said Emily. "I can't let you do this."

"It is done. I won't let you die, Emily. Not because of him."

Samaan lowered the knife and sighed. "Dante, I cannot stop Klanek. I speak the truth."

Dante stood before him, arms out wide. "Then I bid you goodbye, brother, and pray you do better when I am gone."

"This is not what I wanted."

"Then you have learned the lesson many idiots before you have learned. Play with fire and it'll burn you. Your pain is no excuse for evil deeds."

Samaan bowed his head. "Forgive me. Forgive me for my weakness and I shall seek to make amends."

"I do not forgive you, Samaan. You do not deserve mercy."

Samaan flinched. Not being forgiven seemed to hurt him. Emily was glad, but she was too dizzy to enjoy the feeling. The room was spinning.

She gasped and hit the ground, her exhaustion finally winning out.

. . .

Dante helped Emily sit up on the dirty carpet. The feel of the clumped, oily fibres beneath her fingers made her groan. So did the pain in her head. "I... I need water."

Dante glared at Samaan. "Water, now!"

"Do not forget yourself, brother. I am still a servant of the sect."

"And you're still a human being, so get her some water."

With a huff, Samaan left the room. As soon as he was gone, Dante leant in closer to Emily. She thought he was going to kiss her, but he whispered in her ear. "I know what needs to be done. Stay down and do not get involved."

"What? What are you...?"

Samaan re-entered the room and handed Emily a glass of water. She downed it in one, but when she went to hand it back, Dante took it and smashed it over Samaan's head.

Samaan cried out in surprise and stumbled to one knee. "Dante? What did you—"

Dante threw himself at Samaan. They landed on the floor, rolling back and forth. Samaan still had the knife and used it to slash at Dante's neck. Dante grabbed his wrist just in time to stop the blade from kissing his flesh. They struggled back and forth, grunting and cursing.

But Samaan was stronger.

I have to help Dante. He's given up everything for me.

Emily staggered to her feet. She didn't have the strength to pull Samaan off of Dante, so she looked around the room for a weapon. But all she saw were cat skulls and occult paraphernalia.

Gross, gross, gross!

She grabbed the cat skull from the pedestal and weighed it up in her hand. It wasn't heavy, nor was it particularly solid, but not knowing what else to do, she smashed it against the back of Samaan's head. The brittle bone shattered into a hundred pieces.

It was enough to dislodge Samaan.

Dante shoved him aside and rolled onto his feet. He was panting heavily.

Samaan leapt up with the knife.

A shard of bone had remained in Emily's hand, almost in the shape of a dagger. "I have to kill you," she said, more to herself than Samaan. "I'm sorry."

Samaan didn't move out of her way. The bone-handled knife stayed by his side. "It won't save your friends," he told her.

"Killing you will break the curse."

"Not if it is by your hand."

Dante put a hand on her shoulder from behind. He was hot from exertion. "What do you mean, Samaan? Kill a witch and you enfeeble their magic. Is that not correct?"

"Klanek is a being of balance. You are marked for death, Dante, which means you can only break the curse by taking a life in lieu of your own – mine or any other – but this woman is no longer cursed. Her fate has no bearing on the demands of Klanek. If she kills me, then it is a simple murder without consequence."

Dante nodded. "Then the deed will be mine."

Samaan lifted the knife. "Then come, brother. Let us end this."

A gasp sounded from the coffin.

Samaan raced over to his sister, placing a hand inside the box and shushing her. "It is okay, my sweet flower. Soon you will be well. Soon we will be together."

Emani continued to gasp, sucking in air. It sounded like she was suffocating.

Emily eyed the open doorway. She could run. She was no longer cursed.

But Lily and Kaley still are. Dante too.

Dante didn't have a weapon. If he tried to fight Samaan, he could get stabbed. She had to find something for him to defend himself with. Once again, she searched the room and found another skull. This time, she threw it. It missed Samaan but smashed against the wall behind him.

His sister's gasps grew more desperate.

"Stop!" Samaan turned and raged at Emily. "Stop it now, woman!"

Emily frowned. *Stop what? Smashing the skulls?*

Emily turned and grabbed another skull from a pile on the carpet.

"Stop calling me woman!" She threw the skull at Samaan and caused him to duck as it smashed against the wall. She then turned back to the pile and stomped on the gathered bones. They crunched and splintered beneath the sole of her trainer.

Samaan's sister wheezed and spluttered like a dying patient. Air leaked out of her in a tight squeal.

Samaan roared in anguish. He turned and lunged at Emily. "You're killing her!"

Dante moved to meet Samaan's charge, blocking his path to Emily. Meanwhile, she continued smashing skulls around the room. The air filled with the stench of rotting eggs.

The gasps from the coffin strangled to silence.

Samaan bellowed and tried to bury the knife in Dante's neck, but Dante turned and tripped him. As he fell, the knife came free and clattered to the carpet. Samaan immediately went to retrieve it, crawling on his belly, but Dante got to it first.

"It is over, brother." Dante held the blade but did not use it. Instead, he booted Samaan in the ribs and caused him to crease up into a ball. Next, he dropped down on top of the bigger man and straddled him with the knife pointed down at his chest. "I am sorry. This must be done."

"Do it!" Samaan roared, doing nothing to struggle free. In fact, his arms flopped to the side. "I do not care. I shall serve Klanek in the next life."

Dante gritted his teeth, his expression feral – a man about to commit murder.

Emily stood at the back of the room, dusty old curtains

behind her. She wanted to cry out for him to do it, but at the same time she couldn't cheer on a killing. So she said nothing.

Dante held the knife over Samaan's chest.

Samaan still did nothing to fight back.

The knife lowered an inch and stopped.

"I-I can't do it," said Dante. "I can't kill a brother. Even if he deserves it."

"You have to," said Emily. "If you don't, you'll die."

Dante looked back over his shoulder at her. "And what if I end his life? Do I spend the rest of my days in prison, or do I walk free, with my hands soaked in blood? I am sorry, but I cannot commit this sin."

She looked into his eyes and wanted to weep. "Don't be sorry," she said. "I understand."

"Mercy makes you weak," said Samaan.

"No, Samaan, it makes me strong. Stronger than you." He slumped sideways and sat on the dirty carpet with the knife in his lap. "My anger does not control me."

Samaan remained on his back, staring up at the ceiling. "She is gone," he said after a moment. "The ritual to give her life was delicate. You have destroyed it."

Emily looked around the room and at the bone shards covering the carpet. Had they been part of some black magic spell to bring back Samaan's sister?

And I just broke it so she's gone forever.

Samaan got up, but his anger was gone. The violence was over. He bled from his face and was badly out of breath, and when he turned to Dante, he appeared guilty. "This is not what I wanted. I did not ask to be attacked by this woman and her friends, and I did not ask for the hatred this country has shown us simply for existing. Nor did my sweet sister ask to be born in a time of war and brutality. You know why I came here, Dante. I came here to escape the sect. I wanted to walk a fresh path – a path of peace. Allah forgive me, I tried, but this place would not allow me. It beat me and spat at me and judged me. In this country, we are vermin."

Dante nodded. "I know."

"Then you also know the rage inside of me."

"I do." He rubbed at his slashed hand, which was stained red with blood. "But you failed to control that rage, and now it controls you. If you can stop this curse, brother, I beg of you to do so. End this misery you have caused."

"If I could take back what I have done, I would do so. Truly. This is not what I wanted. I… regret my actions."

Dante let his head drop, hands folded in his lap. "Then I suppose that is something."

"What now?" said Emily, still standing at the back of the room. "What happens next?"

Samaan looked at her and sighed. "We wait for Klanek to take what is owed."

CHAPTER
FOURTEEN

DANTE GOT UP. He handed Samaan back his ornate knife and wiped his hands on his long-sleeved T-shirt, staining it with blood from his hand. "Come on," he turned to Emily, "let's get out of here."

"And go where? What if something happens?"

"Then it would be best for you to be away from me. It is late. I need to get you home. In this place it is not safe to be alone."

He's right.

She realised she was in the bad part of town, and if something happened to Dante, she would be stranded there by herself.

It would be morning soon. Her eyelids felt like they had weights attached to them.

"Okay." She took Dante's hand, and they headed for the door. As they walked, bone fragments crunched and rolled beneath their feet.

Dante cried out. His ankle folded as his foot slipped on the bones. He stayed on his feet, but he went colliding into the lamp beside the door and sent it crashing onto the floor. It shattered like the cat skulls had.

A spark of electricity crackled in the air.

A split second later, the mouldy old carpet was on fire.

The flames started small, just a sizzle of smoke and the quivering orange lick of heat. Then they started to spread in every direction, and within seconds, the fire started to eat at the skirting boards and climb up the wall.

"Oh no," said Dante. He stamped at the flames, again and again, but they continued to spread and grow.

Emily yanked him backwards. "Don't! You'll set yourself on fire. We have to get out of here."

Dante watched the flames, mesmerised. Then he checked his hands and arms as if he feared he might be burning.

"We have to go," Emily said again, and she pulled at him harder. "Now, Dante."

He went with her, but turned to face the room. "Samaan, come on."

Samaan was standing by his sister's coffin, staring at the body inside. "She drowned because of me. I promised her it would be safe to come, that a better life was waiting for her at the end of her journey."

Dante stepped towards him. "Samaan, you have to leave here. The fire is spreading too quickly."

Samaan did not turn away from the coffin. He remained exactly where he was. "My time is at an end. I welcome it."

Emily stood in the doorway. If Samaan stayed here and burned, would the curse be broken?

No. Dante needs to be the one to kill him.

And even then, it won't save Lily or Kaley or Harry. They would have to kill someone themselves in order to break their own curses. Or kiss someone to pass it on.

I have to find them. Kaley isn't herself since Ross died. No telling what she might do.

Dante moved towards Samaan, but the carpet in front of him suddenly combusted as the fire moved unnaturally across the room. It was no ordinary blaze. It had purpose.

The flames cut the room off, preventing Dante from getting

to Samaan, so Emily grabbed him and yanked him out into the hallway just as the flames rose up in front of the doorway. A second later and they would have been trapped in a cage of fire.

Samaan turned to face them, dark eyes flickering in the light of the flames. It was still unclear if he regretted his actions fully, but he seemed defiant. Either way, he was about to pay for his sins.

Dante tripped on the bulging floorboards inside the hallway, but Emily kept him from falling. Together, they staggered towards the front door. A veil of black smoke followed them, and so did Samaan's screams as the fire claimed him.

The front door was stuck. Emily panicked. The handle would not budge. But then it gave a little, and she was able to yank it open and let in the cool night air.

The sky was a dark shade of blue, morning on its way.

What time is it?

5AM!

They staggered through the overgrown front garden and onto the road. Once they were far enough away, they turned back to face Samaan's house.

Flames licked the edges of the boarded-up window while the PVC frames around the others were starting to melt. The inferno had taken hold incredibly fast. The flames had even reached the second-floor windows. Pops and cracks echoed inside as wooden beams and plasterboards gave way. Samaan's screams were louder than them all.

Lights switched on inside the other houses as people woke up or were alerted by the noise. A few minutes later, the residents wandered out of their homes to witness the bonfire.

Samaan's screams ceased.

Emily studied the hungry blaze and saw a million shifting shapes. The flames were never still, always consuming.

It's staring back at me. It's a living thing. A spirit of destruction.

Emily knew, right then, at that moment, Klanek was watching them.

She reached out and took Dante's hand. "Kiss me. Kiss me and forget about me."

He ran his bloody hand along her cheek. "I could never forget you, Emily. Perhaps with Samaan gone, this will all be over. We have to hope."

"Samaan said that's not how it works."

"Samaan messed with forces beyond his control. He does not know everything."

"You really think there's a chance?"

He looked around at the neighbours gawping from their front gardens. Many of them wore dressing gowns or pyjamas. "I have to hope," he said. "It's what makes us human."

She leant against him and pulled his arms around her as the house continued to burn. It was perversely romantic, and she had never felt so safe and so in danger at the same time as she did being in Dante's arms. He was right about hope. She needed to hold on to it. Because it was all she had.

Please don't let my friends die. Please don't let Dante die.

The sirens were their cue to leave. Samaan's house was collapsing, the roof caving in and debris raining down in the front garden. The place had been in such a state of disrepair that it had only needed the slightest provocation to fall down.

As they attempted to exit the area, one of the other residents staggered into their path. He was clearly high, bugged eyes rolling all over the place. From his non-existent waistline, it appeared he hadn't eaten in days – nor taken a shower recently if his greasy hair was anything to go by. His hoodie was three sizes too big. "What'a fuck you do?" He slurred at them. "I saw ya. I saw ya coming out of there."

"Please, let us pass," said Dante.

"Who's this bitch?" the junkie asked. "She up for some fun?"

Dante put an arm out to move the man, but he slapped it away.

"Don't fuckin' touch me, mate. I'll nut ya." He winked at Emily. "And then I'll *fuck* her until she loves me."

Emily recoiled in disgust. The thought of this horrible man's dirty fingers on her body… "Get out of our way," she demanded.

"No. I want summin' from ya, or I'll tell the pigs ya set the fire."

"Get out of the way," Dante yelled.

"We can share her, mate. Chill out." The junkie lunged at Emily, but Dante grabbed him around the waist and lifted him with ease. He kicked his legs and swore but couldn't get free. "Lemme go, ya twat."

"I will," said Dante. "When you calm down."

The junkie continued to struggle. He reached into the front of his hoodie.

Emily's eyes went wide. "Dante! He's got something."

The junkie stabbed something into Dante's arm as it remained wrapped around his waist. Immediately, Dante hissed and let go of the man.

"Fuckin' bastard," said the junkie, but blessedly he scurried off back inside his house.

Emily rushed to help Dante. He had his arm out in front of him and was staring at it in horror. Something was protruding from his forearm. A syringe. "Oh God," she said. "Pull it out. Pull it out of your arm."

He swallowed audibly and then held his breath. With a shaking right hand, he clasped the thin glass tube and yanked the needle out of his arm. A bead of blood appeared and ran down the back of his wrist. He lifted the syringe in front of him and gave it a little shake. There was a small amount of dirty brown liquid at the bottom. Disgusted, he turned and threw it into the junkie's front garden.

"Did he inject you?" asked Emily. "Did any of that stuff get in you?"

"I… I don't know. I think I'm okay."

Not if that junkie has hepatitis or HIV.

If Dante lives long enough to catch a disease, then maybe that's a win.

I need to find out if Kaley and Lily and Harry are okay.

Dante was staring past her. The junkie had reappeared with two friends, and the three of them were standing in the doorway of the house, pointing and conspiring.

"We need to go," he said. "We're drawing a lot of attention."

Emily saw more residents staring at them, and the fire engines were getting close. This really wasn't somewhere where they wanted to hang around. She took his hand and they entered a swift jog as she felt eyes on the back of her head.

They were fleeing the scene of a crime.

The residents might not be big fans of authority, but Samaan had been their neighbour. And now he was dead.

And he deserved it. Ross and Matt are gone because of him.

So why don't I feel any satisfaction?

They kept on hurrying until they were out of the close, and then carried on further until they found a small green with a park bench. Emily had to stop to take a rest. Her ribs were full of pins, and her knees kept buckling as she walked. The tiredness was so overwhelming that it made her dizzy – and sick. Dante slumped down beside her, obviously shattered himself.

She reached out and put a hand on his leg. "We're going to be in so much trouble."

He put his hand on top of hers. "No. The p-people around here don't give the police answers. They are angry, but they won't identify usss. They won't want the bother of it."

"But… didn't they all know Samaan?"

"Perhapsss. He kept much to himself, s-s-so I doubt he had many… many friends among his neighbours. It'll be okay."

His words were slurring. Emily turned to look at him and saw that his pupils had enlarged. "Shit! That junk got inside you, Dante. Are you okay?"

He smiled. "I feel fine. I just need to rest a minute."

She nodded. "Okay. Um, we should go to the hospital when you're ready."

"Yeah, maybe. In a… minute."

"I'm so sorry. I… I can't believe this is happening. It's like a nightmare. Do you think I'm a bad person?"

"No!" He squeezed her hand as it rested in his lap. His words continued to slur, but now that he was aware of it, he controlled it a little. "You are beautiful and kind. You remind me of my mother."

She frowned. "Is that good?"

"She had a kind heart too. When times got hard in Syria, she baked bread for the local children. Many did not eat enough, so she did what she could to help them. Soon, people in our village started to donate flour and other supplies to help her make more. She became known as the Lady Baker." He smiled, the memory clearly pleasing to him. "My father… he worked hard to give her the freedom to do as she wished, but she chose to use her time to help others. I was the most popular little boy in town because of… because of my mother."

Emily chuckled. "All my mum ever did was embarrass me as a kid, but now I'm older, I see how lucky I am to have her. She loves me with all her heart."

He didn't seem to hear her. "My mother and father were driving to see relatives in another village when a missile struck the local hotel. It was the tallest building in the area, four storeys high, and it toppled over onto the road. My parents might have been alive for a while, buried in the rubble, but by the time the villagers pulled them out, they were cold."

"Dante… That's horrible. I'm so sorry. Was it… was it us that sent the missile?"

He looked at her with bleary eyes. "You do not know about the war in my homeland, do you?"

She shook her head and suddenly felt ashamed. "The news only ever depresses me. I know it was bad in Syria for a while."

"It wasn't your people that sent the missile. Syrians fight

Syrians where I come from. That is the biggest pain of it. When I left my country I was twelve years old. I travelled with an older friend, but I lost him somewhere in France. I believe… I believe I became a burden to him, although I had taken all of my parent's savings and p-paid my own way. Eventually… I made my way to the UK."

"Why here? I don't have a problem with it or anything, I just want to know."

He shrugged. His slurred words had now taken on a sleepy quality. "For many of the reasons you probably think, and several that you don't. I cannot speak French, and my parents got me an English tutor when I was young, so… so it made sense for me to come here. There is also an understanding that the people in the UK are welcoming, and that your government is honest and humane."

She pulled a face. "Boy, did you hear wrong."

"Perhaps. The truth is not so far away. The UK is not perfect, but… nor is anywhere else. Anyway… Anyway, I applied to settle here and was accepted. Getting work was a struggle, b-but I have had s-several jobs and have done my b-best. It is hard, with no… education." His eyes closed, and he tilted slightly towards her.

"Hey! Hey, Dante, stay with me. Don't go to sleep."

"I am just resting."

"No. Shit! I need to call an ambulance."

He opened his eyes and shook his head. "No! If I am found with drugs in my system they might report it to the police. I can't be branded a criminal."

"But we don't know what was in that syringe."

"Probably heroin. Please, do not call help."

She nodded, but it felt wrong. "I'm glad I met you, Dante. It's opened my eyes. Before, I looked at migrants as a different species. I would avoid people like you. I assumed you were all criminals or benefit seekers. Why didn't I ever think of you as individuals? I guess Harry isn't the only racist, huh? Whatever happens from now on, I'm going to do better. John can stuff his job up his arse, too, because life is too short to waste. You've shown me that people have it far worse than I do, and if your mum could spend her days helping people, then so can we all. I'm going to do better, Dante, I promise. Dante?"

He was sitting with a smile on his face, staring at the houses in the distance.

She squeezed his hand, but he didn't squeeze back. She pulled her arm free and prodded him in the ribs. "Dante? Say something."

He slumped back against the bench, his head tipping back. His eyes were like glass orbs. Frothy spittle drooled from his mouth.

"No, no, no..." She shook him over and over, but his body flopped about like a rag doll. All the life inside of him was gone. Klanek had collected.

This is all my fault. He was trying to protect me.
I should be the one who's dead.

She grabbed him by the shoulders and shoved her lips against his, kissing him hard. She pulled away and moaned. "Give it back to me. Let me be the one to die." She kissed him again, lingering, and praying that the curse would come back to her. It was what she deserved.

But eventually she had no choice but to let Dante rest. She placed him upright on the bench and placed his hands in his lap. To a passer-by he would look to be sitting peacefully. A handsome young boy with his whole life ahead of him.

She then staggered onto the grass and retched, the manky old chicken finally coming up and splattering her feet. "I hope your mum and dad are waiting for you, Dante. I'm so sorry."

She walked away, leaving behind the young man who had given his life for hers.

CHAPTER
FIFTEEN

EMILY WANDERED unrecognisable through street after unrecognisable street, a zombie with a slow-beating pulse. With the arrival of dawn, cars repopulated the roads, and front doors opened and closed as people went miserably to start work on a Monday. The rising sun should have made her feel safer, but it didn't. The dangers of night might have gone to bed, but daylight couldn't protect her from a poisoned fate.

Sure enough, when Emily considered catching a bus, she realised her jeans pocket had a hole in it, and that all of her change had slipped away unseen. Then it started to rain, and even with Dante's jumper, she shivered. The final straw was when she ripped her trainer on a tree root poking out of the pavement. Her luck was still rotten. Klanek was toying with her, softening her up before decapitating her like Matt or cracking open her skull like Ross.

Why did I kiss Dante? I took away any reason for him to have sacrificed himself. He died for nothing.

Emily stared up at the grey sky that should have been bright blue and filled with summer sunshine. She tried to let the rain drown her. It didn't, of course, and all it did was make her eyes sting. Enraged, she yelled at God for not answering her prayers.

"If you're real, then why are you letting this happen? Why do you let monsters like Klanek exist? Are you too weak to help me?"

As she stood in the rain, staring up at the sky, she realised someone was watching her from their driveway. Surprisingly, she was still able to feel embarrassment, so to get away from prying eyes, she followed a path into a nearby wooded area. Perhaps a tree would fall down and kill her.

"Come on, you son of a bitch. Get it over with. I don't even care any more. I'm tired, and my friends are dead, so just kill me." She stepped off the path and dropped to her knees in the grass. "I'm done. I... can't go on."

Something moved in a nearby thicket.

A serial killer with a knife? A rabid dog on the loose? Maybe even an unexploded bomb from World War Two shifting in the soil and about to go off.

What she didn't expect to see was a cat.

A black cat. Maybe the same one she had seen twice already.

It's part of this. It's following me.

Were black cats unlucky or lucky? She couldn't quite remember. What she did know was that this black spectre had been present since Ross's accident, watching from the shadows.

Emily took a step towards the cat. It was sitting on a plot of grass filling a space between two blocks of housing, showing no sign of concern that she was approaching. Its tail swished lazily in the air.

"What do you want?" she yelled. "Why are you following me? Are you Klanek?"

The cat stared at her. It didn't look like a demon, nor did it appear to understand her. It looked like an ordinary cat.

When she got within ten feet of it, the animal turned briskly and trotted off with its tail in the air. It did not run, so Emily followed after it, ready to sprint if it tried to escape. The way she was feeling right now, she was ready to wring its neck.

"Where are you going? Stop and face me." She didn't feel

crazy for shouting at a cat, which in itself was probably quite crazy. With the lack of sleep and massive amounts of trauma she'd endured, the situation felt totally normal.

The cat slunk off towards some bushes. If Emily wasn't quick, it might disappear into the thicket and end her pursuit. But it stopped short and turned around to face her, looking her right in the eye.

Emily slowed to a halt, goose pimples popping up along her arms. She looked back and saw the pathway twenty metres behind, and no people in the vicinity. Was this it? Had this cat led her away to kill her through some terrible means? Was something going to leap out of the bushes and grab her?

Nothing happened.

The cat remained where it was, looking her in the eyes.

She took a step towards it. Then a second. Its tail swished back and forth.

"What are you doing? Why did you lead me over here?" She looked around suspiciously. "What's the trick?"

The cat lowered down onto its front paws and tucked them underneath itself. Any ordinary cat would have been concerned by a stranger's proximity, but this one almost seemed to ignore her. It sniffed at the grass.

What is that?

She noticed something. A small object of a slightly lighter green hue. The cat was nosing it and licking its lips. It was some kind of weed.

No, not a weed... That's a four-leaf clover.

Emily cautiously knelt in front of the cat. She reached out a hand and carefully touched the top of its head. It didn't flinch or shy away, so she stroked its silky fur. "Are you trying to help me? Are you not... Klanek."

The cat hissed.

"I'll take that as a no. Who are you then?"

The cat stood, turned around, and ducked into the bushes. It obviously wasn't in the mood for conversation.

Emily studied the tiny four-leaf clover sticking out of the grass. It couldn't be a coincidence; the cat had led her right to it. "I could really do with the luck of the Irish," she said and, not knowing what else to do, plucked it out of the ground. It was probably her imagination, but she suddenly felt a little better. Safer, perhaps. Or was she just hopeful?

She placed the clover into the shirt pocket of her work shirt and gave it a gentle pat.

Will it keep me safe? Is it that simple? Can it keep Kaley and Lily safe, too?

I need to find them before it's too late.

She hurried back towards the pathway.

Kaley, Lily, and Harry had all texted Emily a dozen times each. They were still at the beach, having huddled together at the Rock to stay warm and safe, and all were relieved when Emily finally texted back. Lily begged her to come join them.

So she did.

Getting out of the area where Dante had brought her was confusing at first, but once she found a main road she was able to follow signs to the seafront. It took almost an hour, and when she reached the Rock, the sun had risen over the sea and the tide was almost all the way in, leaving her friends stranded on top of the stony outcropping. Luckily, you could climb on and off of the Rock from the promenade with the aid of a small hop.

Emily, however, decided hopping wasn't worth the risk, so she waited on the promenade until her friends joined her.

Lily threw her arms around her. "I've been here all night worrying about you. Thank God you're okay."

"I wouldn't go that far. It's been a rough few hours."

"Yeah." Lily let out a sigh. "They closed off the entire street where Matt died."

Emily felt sick at the memory of her childhood friend spread across the road, so she twisted her fingers to keep the pain physical instead of mental. "Did the police not grab you all?"

"We ran," said Harry, folding his arms as he leant against the low stone wall. "We were all so freaked that we just legged it right after you did. The coppers are going to be looking for answers though, for sure. Fuck knows what we tell 'em."

"But the road sweeper will say it was an accident, right?"

"I doubt he even understands what happened. It was like something out of a horror movie." He shook his head with a tired huff. "He was my best mate. I can't believe he's gone."

"Do you know if we're still cursed?" Kaley asked Emily. She was also sitting on the stone wall that ran alongside the promenade. "We haven't moved from here, but nothing's happened. We've been hoping everything is okay again."

"It's not," said Emily. "A lot has happened, but the curse is still active."

Harry frowned at her. "How do you know for sure?"

"Because I met up with Dante and we went to go see Samaan at his house."

Lily gasped. "Did you get him to stop the curse?"

"No, he couldn't do it. He's dead now. His house burned down. Dante's dead, too."

Lily paced back and forth. There were dark circles under her eyes and her pale make-up had smudged. Bruising from her forehead had spread down the entire left side of her face. When she looked at Emily, she appeared half-crazed. "What the hell, Ems? How are they both dead? They weren't even cursed."

"Dante was. He took it from me. That's what caused the fire that burned Samaan to death, and why Dante died right afterwards from an accidental overdose."

Kaley's forehead creased. "Overdose?"

"Wait," said Harry, putting a finger up in front of his nose. "Did you say Dante took the curse from you? How? Are you… are you wearing his jumper?"

"He took the curse away by kissing me. Samaan told us you can pass the curse on by doing that and—"

Out of the blue, Harry grabbed Emily by the back of the head and planted a kiss on her mouth. She tried to push him away, but he held her in place, crushing their lips together. It wasn't until she elbowed him in the ribs that he finally let go. "What the fuck, Harry? What are you doing?"

"Is that it?" he said. "Have I got rid of it?"

She realised what he was trying to do, and she couldn't hide her disgust. "Y-You just tried to pass your curse onto me? You pathetic bastard!"

"Did it work?"

She sneered and took great pleasure in telling him no. "I kissed him and took it back. I still have bad luck."

At least I did until I found the clover. Nothing happened on my way here.

Harry glared at her, fists clenched. "What? Why would you do that? Are you fucking stupid?"

Lil pulled at her hair. "You were safe and you took it back? Why?"

"I don't know why I did it. Guilt, probably. Dante gave his life to save me."

Harry sneered. "Did you two shag or something? It's disgusting how you've been sniffing around that lowlife every time our backs are turned."

Emily stepped forward and looked him right in the eye. "You're the only lowlife, Harry. You're a racist piece of shit, and I wish none of us had ever met you. This all started because of the violence *you* caused. Dante only ever tried to help us. Now he's gone."

"Too bad. He could have made you one of his wives."

Kaley tutted, a look of disgust on her face. "Just shut the hell up, Harry. She's right, you *are a* racist."

"No, I ain't. I just don't like foreign invaders coming here and taking the piss. Is that so wrong?"

Emily pointed a finger at his face. "Dante was ten times the man you are. He lost his parents, his country, his future, and he still didn't give in to anger and pettiness like you. He was a good man and you're a worthless prick."

She didn't expect him to hit her.

Harry slapped her across the face, knocking her to the pavement. He stood over her, spitting with rage. "Who do you think you're fucking talking to?"

Cars zipped back and forth on the main road, but none stopped to help. He'd just struck her in broad daylight, but no one cared. Kaley and Lily, however, yelled furiously and raced to protect Emily, but Harry threatened to hit them too.

Emily put a hand to her lip and tasted blood. "You've lost your damn mind."

He leant over her and growled. "I'm not the one kissing dirty asylum seekers. I can't believe I was ever interested in a slag like you."

Emily had never spat at anyone before, but she hit the target first time. Bloody saliva leaked down Harry's face, and his expression contorted like a broken mirror. For a split second, he looked just like Samaan had when he had cursed them all.

"Bitch!" He grabbed her by the hair and started yanking her along the pavement, her legs kicking left and right. "If we're all going to die," he said, "then I might as well enjoy myself. I'll do you a favour and get it over with quick."

Emily squealed as her scalp pulled away from her skull. It felt like fire ants in her hair. "Get off me!"

"Get off her!" Lily and Kaley grabbed Harry by the arms and yanked him backwards. He lost his grip on Emily, but a bunch of her blonde hair tore free and ended up in his fist.

"Don't touch me," he roared at the girls as they struggled to keep a hold of his arms. He thrashed and whipped himself back and forth, sending both of them staggering. Kaley lost her footing and fell down, but Lily held on for dear life. "You touch her again and I'll kill you," she roared. "You fucking bastard."

Harry shoved Lily backwards against the stone wall. She almost toppled over it but managed to drop and sit down instead. Harry sneered at her and shook his head. His face was bright red with fury. "She's never gonna fuck you, you know?"

Emily was still on the ground. The shock from the blow had worn off, but her legs were heavy and she didn't want to get up. "Leave her alone, Harry."

He turned to her and smirked. "You know what Lily told me after we were done screwing last week?"

"Don't!" Lily shook her head at him. "Please."

"She said she was bi and that she's been in love with you for ages. I found it kind of hot at the time. Now it's just sad."

"You bastard!" Lily sobbed.

"It's okay," said Emily, smiling at her friend. "You're my favourite person in the whole world, Lil."

Harry sucked in air and grimaced. "Ouch! Sounds like you just got friend zoned, babes."

"Fuck you!" Lily rushed at Harry with her claws out, aiming for his eyes.

Instead of trying to avoid her, he shoved her in the chest with both hands.

Lily went hurtling backwards, much harder than before. Her thighs hit the low stone wall and momentum sent her up and over. She shrieked and threw out a hand. But it was in vain.

Time seemed to slow down. Emily looked into Lily's terrified eyes and reached for her, but she was too far away. Too far away and falling backwards through the air.

Then she was gone.

"Lily!" Emily leapt up and ran to the wall. She almost went right over herself, but sprawled across the top. The fall was only six or seven feet. Not a lethal drop.

But Lily was dead.

Emily shook her head, wishing she could change reality by disbelieving in it hard enough. "No, no, no."

Lily was face down on the beach, but her head was on backwards. Her neck had snapped like a twig and twisted completely around. She had landed in the worst way possible because of bad luck.

Kaley slumped onto the wall beside Emily and stared in stunned silence.

Lily's eyes were open, and her mouth was curled almost into a smile. If not for her head facing the wrong way, she might have seemed normal.

"I love you," said Emily. "Always."

She clenched her fists and turned around. Harry had lost all colour from his face, clearly not having meant to have pushed her over the wall, just like Samaan hadn't meant to unleash Klanek. Their anger was to blame. For everything. And there was zero excuse. "I'm going to kill you," she said. "I'm going to tear you apart."

CHAPTER
SIXTEEN

EMILY SHOVED Harry towards the road, hoping he would stumble into traffic. But he was much stronger than her, and all she did was push him back a step. For a moment he seemed lost, but then he turned on her, forcing her back towards the stone wall. She was powerless as he lifted her over the top and held her by her neck as she dangled helplessly over Lily's corpse.

Who will find her body? A dog walker? A child?

We need to call the police.

And tell them what? How do we explain that three of our friends died in one night? Plus two young Syrian men.

I don't need to tell them anything, because I'll be dead soon.

"Do it!" she said. "At least I know I won't end up in hell like you."

"I ain't dying. You told me what I need to do." He squeezed her throat, choking the life out of her. She almost didn't care, but the thought of her mum's tears forced her to fight back. With a last gasp, she reached out and prodded his black eye. Then she raked his cheek with her nails.

He reeled back, clutching his face and hissing. It gave her

time to push herself away from the wall and back onto the safety of the pavement. "Get away from me."

"Bitch!" He took a step towards her, but Kaley charged into him and told him to get lost.

"Get the hell out of here before I claw your eyes out, you bastard."

To Emily's relief, Harry chose not to fight any longer, and he took off down the promenade at a run, yelling obscenities as he departed. *Good riddance.*

Kaley moved to Emily and hugged her. "What do we do now? Lily…"

"We need to go somewhere before they find her body. If we get taken in by the police we'll have no chance of surviving."

"What chance do we have anyway?"

"Not much, but I changed my luck earlier by doing lucky things. Maybe that's the key. We need to curse ourselves with good luck."

Kaley frowned. "I don't understand. How do we do that?"

"We touch wood every time we see it. We don't step on cracks or walk under ladders. Maybe we get some salt and throw it over our shoulder every few steps." She reached into her pocket and pulled out the four-leaf clover. "Oh, and you hold on to this. It's kept me safe since I found it. Now it's going to do the same for you."

Kaley frowned, but she carefully took it and examined it. "You really think this will make a difference?"

She nodded. "We can change our luck by doing the things I just said."

"But for how long? Our entire lives? We'll go insane."

Emily held Kaley's hands and looked her in the eye. "It's just to buy us some time."

"Time to do what?"

"To find a permanent way to end this. If it's all down to black magic and demons, we can fight back. There're rules we can make use of."

"Like what? Kissing people?"

Emily nodded. "If it comes to it, yeah. Kissing someone will pass on the curse. And there's something else."

"What?"

She took a breath, not knowing if she should share the information. Then she reminded herself who she was talking to. Kaley, one of her oldest friends, future human rights lawyer. "If we take a life, it removes our mark."

"Our mark?"

"The curse. If we kill someone, they take our place. Samaan told me before he burned."

Kaley shook her head over and over, starting to panic. "I can't kill anyone, Ems. I can't."

Emily grabbed her by the arms and shook her. "We're going to do whatever we have to. Either that or we die. Do you want to die?"

"N-No."

"Then we need to beat this."

"It's already taken Ross, Matt, and Lily. How can we can beat it when they couldn't?"

Emily sighed and hugged her. "Can you just go with my motivational speech, please, babes? All we can do is hope. Without that, we're doomed."

Kaley wiped a tear from her eye and nodded. "Okay, we're going to beat this thing. You and me."

"Keep hold of that clover and you'll be fine."

"But what about you?"

Emily smiled. "I have an idea. It's almost nine o'clock and businesses are about to open, right? You got your bank card on you?"

"Yeah, why?"

"Because we're going to go buy ourselves some luck."

Kaley frowned, not understanding, but once Emily explained, it started to make sense to her. "My family will kill me," she said.

"You'd better hide it then. If you don't do it, you might be dead anyway."

"Good point."

Emily smiled. "So, you game?"

"I just hope it doesn't hurt too much. You'll be there, right?"

"Of course. Come on, let's go get it over with."

The man behind the desk had seemed surprised to find two girls queuing outside when he had opened up his doors. Fortunately, his first appointment wasn't until ten thirty, so he could fit them in.

Emily had always wanted a tattoo, but she hadn't figured on getting a bunch of four-leaf clovers inked onto her shoulder. People would forever assume she was Irish, but she would take that happily if it meant not dying. Along with the clovers, she had a pair of dice – sixes up – put on her tummy too. She didn't know if it would be enough to keep her safe, but it was something at least.

Kaley was squeamish about needles, but the young, heavily pierced artist did a lot to put her at ease, joking with her and telling her how pretty she was. Emily clasped her hand the whole time. Once it was over, Kaley had a tiny four-leaf clover tucked secretively behind her left ear and a rabbit's foot on the inside of her thigh. Both images were crisp, colourful, and expertly done, but it was obvious the artists found the whole thing weird. Several times he asked why they wanted lucky symbols on their bodies, and several times they shrugged it off by saying it was personal. He didn't press them. Being nosy wasn't part of his job.

When they stepped outside the shop, a sunny day met them. People occupied the pavements and cars filled the roads. The busyness made Emily worry. It was hard to keep an eye on everything when so much was moving, but as she stuck close to Kaley, she felt a little better. Maybe the tattoos would keep them safe and it would finally be over. Maybe they would do nothing. For now, at least, they were alive, and neither of them was giving up.

There were police everywhere. Some directed traffic away from the closed-off main road where Matt's remains coated the asphalt. Others questioned shop owners on the high street. Clearly, they wanted to know what had happened in the middle of the night, and very soon they would come across Lily's body, which would only add fuel to their investigation. Emily's stomach was an ice block of dread.

What if we break the curse only to go to prison for the rest of our lives? Can we be blamed for Matt and Lily? What if Samaan's neighbours identify me? Dante can't have known for sure that they won't.

Dante…

How can I miss you when I barely knew you?

"You doing okay?" she asked Kaley, desperate to keep her mind from wandering.

"I'm okay. I just wish we had a plan. Where do we go now?"

"I'm thinking about it. I'll figure something out. Just trust me."

"I do trust you. Should we… Should we kiss someone? Maybe someone bad, or old?"

Emily sighed. She'd been thinking along the same lines. "Maybe. It could be the only way, but if we go that route we have to be sure. It'll stay with us forever."

"It'll be murder, I know." She took a deep breath and let it out. "I know."

They continued walking in silence for a few minutes, moving through the small crowds that formed outside the larger shops like Primark and Boots. Whenever they saw a police officer they ducked and tried to stay out of sight. They didn't stop until they passed Wetherspoons.

They saw Harry inside.

The pub was busy as usual – one of the cheapest places on the high street to get breakfast – but it wasn't so busy that the staff couldn't stand around chatting to the customers. One member of staff – a young blonde girl probably not yet twenty – was blushing and giggling as Harry leant over the bar and touched her arm, flirting with her, buttering her up.

For a kiss. He's happy to let an innocent girl die in his place.

Kaley shook her head in disgust. "We have to stop him."

"You're right, we do."

Kaley went to go inside, but Emily pulled her back. "No. Not this way. All we'll do is send him racing on to the next place. We need to think about this. If he kisses someone, then he'll be free and some poor girl will die."

CHAPTER
SEVENTEEN

MORE AND MORE POLICE FILLED THE town centre, and Emily was getting frantic text messages from her mum. It was too risky to be in the area, so she and Kaley took cover at the far end of the lower beach, where the sand narrowed and gave way to ten-foot cliffs with an old Roman ruin on top. It was a popular place for hikers, but little else. Hopefully, they would have privacy for what happened next.

There was a bench halfway up a rocky hill that led to the clifftop, and that was where Kaley and Emily waited for Harry. She had texted him and offered peace, claiming she had kissed a random lad and passed on the curse, and that they now needed to stick together to deal with whatever questions came from the police. After a few back-and-forth messages, she had even hinted at a reconciliation. Harry was so full of himself that he actually seemed to believe her, and that she might still be interested in him.

As if I would go anywhere near a racist woman-beating psychopath like you.

"You sure this will work?" said Kaley as she sat down on the bench. She pulled up her injured foot and rubbed around her ankle.

Emily was standing a few feet away. She turned now and smiled. "He's going to fall for it. He probably thinks I'm in love with him."

"We really never should've been friends with him, huh?"

"How could we have known?"

Kaley huffed. "I knew. He gave me bad vibes from the start. Being a minority, you kinda get a sixth sense for it, you know?"

"So why didn't you say anything?"

"I don't know." She shrugged. "You all seemed to like him, and I didn't want you to think I had a chip on my shoulder. It's hard to cry racist in a room full of white faces. I guess I hoped you would all realise it for yourselves eventually. You did."

Emily folded her arms and winced as she pulled the skin taut on her shoulder where her fresh tattoo was. "Not soon enough. I'm sorry if…"

"If what?"

"If I've ever been insensitive about race. To be honest, I've never really thought much about it, and maybe that's the problem."

Kaley shook her head. "You're not part of the problem, Ems, so don't worry. I'm British and I'm Sikh, but before that I'm just plain old Kaley, and you're my friend. You've only ever had my back."

"Are you okay? I know losing Ross was… hard."

"This is been hard on us both. Tell you the truth, I don't even know what I'm feeling. One minute I want to cry, the next I want to kill someone. Mostly, I just want to sleep."

"I hear that!" Emily took a seat beside Kaley and gave her legs a rest, wondering how long she could go without sleep. She decided she was in no hurry to test the limits. It already felt like she was sprinting ever closer to a heart attack – or a nervous breakdown.

They sat in silence for quite some time. Harry arrived at eleven o'clock. From the way he swaggered up the hill to meet them, it was obvious he had fallen for their ploy. He was there to reconcile and get his ducks in a row for the police.

"Ladies, I've missed you. Thought you'd be dead by now."

Emily smiled, although it took great effort even to look at him. His floppy blond hair was no longer attractive; it was downright annoying. "We were worrying the same thing about you. I'm glad you're okay." She unbuttoned her work shirt, pulled it off her shoulder, and peeled off the cotton pad to reveal her tattoo. "We found a way to keep safe until we could find someone to kiss."

He raised an eyebrow at her. "You really passed on your curse?"

She nodded. "Kaley has a nan in the old people's home on Cosgrove Road. It's crazy how easy it is to give a senile old man a goodbye kiss."

"Nice." He smirked with genuine amusement. "Gotta do what you gotta do, right? I planted one on some barmaid down at 'Spoons. Was even easier than I thought it'd be."

It took everything she had not to show how much she detested him, or how disappointed she was to hear that the poor girl from earlier was now cursed.

We should have done something. I stopped Kaley from going in.

Harry nodded to Kaley, who was still sitting on the bench and resting her foot. "How about you? You plant a smacker on your nan?"

"No. I kissed an old woman in the next room. She was in a coma."

"Smart. Don't want to go killing your own family now, do you?"

Kaley's expression slipped a little. "Don't you feel guilty? You picked a young girl, right? Don't you care?"

"No. Why would I? I don't care about some stranger. People die every day. Long as it ain't me, I'm happy."

Emily nodded. "It sucks, but it's true. When it comes down

to us or someone else, there's no choice. Not really. Anyone who says different is a liar."

Harry crunched his way up the rocky hill to join her, with a look on his face that he probably thought of as smouldering. "So we gonna forget about earlier, yeah? Things got a little heated, but stuff gets said in the heat of the moment. I can move on if you can."

Emily stepped forward to meet him. "We need to stick together, so yeah. There's going to be a shitstorm and we need to get our stories straight. What do we say to the police? My mum is calling constantly. I think they've been in contact."

He nodded, and some of his swagger faded. "My old man's been calling too. If the police have been around my gaff, he's gonna kick off big time."

"You know, from the way you talk about your dad, he sounds like a complete arsehole."

"Nah, he's just old school. A proper geezer, you know? Don't like the pigs one bit."

"Nor people with brown faces I'll bet," said Kaley. "Like father like son, huh?"

Emily bit her lip. *Cool it, Kay. This isn't part of the plan. We need to play nice. Get him to trust us.*

Harry shrugged apologetically. "He believes Britain should be for the British. India was part of the empire, so your people had a right to come here. Same as Ross's. I know you think I'm racist, but I ain't."

Kaley chuckled. "My *people*? Do you think we're a different species or something?"

"Yeah, I do. People are different. Why pretend otherwise?"

Emily turned and made eye contact with Kaley, trying to beam a message between them telepathically. *Chill out. Back off.*

Kaley sighed, her combative body language fading. "I guess you're right. My parents hate people from Pakistan, so I guess we have something in common."

"I didn't come here to fight with you two," said Harry, and

he put his hands up in supplication. "Before all this shit went down, we were tight. We shouldn't hold grudges about what happened. Evil curses aren't exactly everyday circumstances, are they?"

"You're right," said Emily. "I'm sorry things got crazy. Look, nothing happened between me and Dante. I was just trying to find a way out of this. And it worked! If not for him, I never would have found out about passing on the curse with a kiss."

Harry nodded. "Yeah, I guess he saved our bacon. If you say nothing happened, then I believe you. Sorry for getting on your back about it."

"No, I'm sorry." She felt sick at the sound of her own words. Being duplicitous had never been a talent of hers, and it disturbed her how well she was managing it right now. "I thought we had something. If it wasn't for all of this…" She shook her head, looked down at the ground. "Can we just forget the last twenty-four hours? Can we go back to holding hands and getting to know each other?"

He gave her the warmest smile; so warm that she almost let it disarm her. He was a monster, but a handsome one. "That's all I want, Ems."

She smiled back and moved up against him. His body was hot against hers, but she felt a chill run through her. She put a hand on his neck as he wrapped an arm around her back, looking into those light blue eyes of his and thinking about her friends. The reality of never seeing Ross, or Matt, or Lily ever again shook her soul, but she swallowed down her grief and pushed herself closer to Harry. "God, you are so fit."

"You're all right yourself."

She tilted her head and went in for a kiss.

Taste my curse, you piece of shit.

Harry moved his mouth towards hers.

He dodged to the side, his mouth beside her ear. "You think I'm stupid, you dumb bitch?"

Emily pulled back, frowning. She opened her mouth to

speak, but only air came out as Harry punched her hard in the stomach. She crumpled to her knees, unable to breathe. It felt like dying. Drowning in the open air. Try as she might, her lungs would not function.

Harry stood over her and snarled. "Do you think for one minute I was going to fall for this bullshit? The only reason I came was to see whatever silly little plan you'd come up with, but you thought you could wave your tits at me and I would kiss you?" He let out a cackle. "Trust me, I ain't about to catch what you've got, sweetheart."

"What about me?"

Harry turned just in time to see Kaley launch herself at him. He caught her in both arms, almost like she was an excited toddler leaping at her dad, but he was too surprised to stop her from doing what she was doing. With both hands, she grabbed the back of his head and planted a smacker on his lips. Harry let out a moan, trying to dislodge her, but she wrapped her entire body around him and squeezed like a python.

Harry squealed.

Suffocating on her knees, Emily realised Kaley had gone from kissing to biting.

Good on your babes.

I'm going to die. I can't breathe. I can't...

Air rushed into Emily's lungs so violently that it almost tore her open. She gasped inwardly, a strangled sound like a whale dying, but then, for a second, she could not breath out again. The battle went on for several more seconds, her diaphragm spasming, dancing between life and death. She saw stars. Darkness encroached upon the edges of her vision.

And then she was breathing again, sucking in air.

She was alive.

Harry roared in anger and tossed Kaley to the ground. She landed on the grassy hill and grunted, as she, too, lost her breath. But she was smiling, bloody around her mouth.

Harry's bottom lip was a mess, split in two on the left-hand side. He staggered back and forth in shock, angry but unfocused. He swore and cursed and wept in equal measure.

Who's gonna kiss you now?

Emily rolled onto her side and probed the rocky ground with her fingers, eventually grabbing hold of a rock embedded in the earth. It was the size of her fist, but it came out of the mud easily, leaving a perfectly smooth depression. It felt good in her hand. Solid.

"You fucking bitches!" Harry roared. "I'll kill you both."

Emily got to her feet slowly, her ribs hot with agony. All three of them were injured, and all three of them groaned in their own misery. Emily was the only one who was focused on anything else.

She marched towards Harry, finding her feet, finding her balance. Finding herself.

He looked up just in time to see her coming.

She raised the rock above her head and swung it. It smashed into Harry's mouth and crushed his lips, probably cracked a tooth or three. He reeled back, squealing like a pig as blood gushed from his mouth. His upper lip was already swelling like a bee had stung him, but now it leaked blood like a bubbling red geyser.

"You're screwed," she shouted. "Kaley gave you her curse, and now no one will ever kiss you. Maybe if you can survive a fortnight your face will heal enough to let your mum kiss you, but I reckon you'll probably be dead by lunchtime."

"You bwitch! You wucking bwitch!" He staggered towards her, but she held the stone aloft and warned him away. At the same time, Kaley leapt up and stood next to her. Together, they were more than capable of dealing with Harry.

"Fuck off and die," said Kaley. "The world has no place for small-minded bullies like you."

"Paki bitch!"

Kaley looked at Emily and rolled her eyes. "Can you believe this idiot?"

"No, I really can't. We should teach him a lesson."

The two of them raced forward to attack. Kaley beat her fists against Harry's ribs like a woman possessed, while Emily smashed the rock against the side of his head again and again, until he had no choice but to turn tail and run, bleeding profusely from his ruined mouth and clutching at growing lumps on his head. "I'll kwill you bwitches," he yelled, but he sounded like a child having a tantrum.

Emily yelled after him. "See ya, Harry. And good luck!"

Once he reached the bottom of the hill, Emily and Kaley both collapsed onto the ground. They lay there for a while, staring at the perfect blue sky.

"So am I okay now?" said Kaley, still lying on her back. "Harry has my curse?"

"If what Samaan told me is true, then yes. I really hope so."

Kaley sat up and looked at Emily. "But you're still in danger. We have to figure out a way to help you too."

"We will. I'm just glad you're okay."

Kaley rummaged in her pockets and pulled out the four-leaf clover. It was flat, and a little ragged, but still intact. She slid it into Emily's breast pocket. "You need this more than me."

"Thanks."

"Hey, the story we gave to Harry wasn't such a bad idea. Maybe we should go to the hospital and kiss someone in a coma or dying of cancer. Or we could find a prison!"

Emily sat up and rubbed at her eyes. She'd been falling asleep mid-conversation. "Maybe. First, we have to help the girl that Harry kissed. She has no idea what he's done to her."

"Well, the floozy shouldn't be kissing guys at nine o'clock in the morning, should she?" Kaley shook her head. "Wow, that was mean of me. I'm tired and all my friends are dead. It's put me in a bad mood."

"Not all of them are," said Emily, giving a thin-lipped smile.

"But I get what you mean. Things will never be the same after this, will they?"

"No. No, they won't, Ems. We won't ever get to go back to our normal lives."

"Do you have any change on you?"

Kaley frowned. "Yeah, I think so. Why?"

"We need to test your luck."

"Like back at the church? That turned out badly."

Emily rolled up onto her knees and beckoned for Kaley to hand over some coins. "It's the only thing I can think of."

Kaley fumbled in her pocket and then handed Emily a pound. She flipped it up and caught it in her palm. "Call it."

"Tails."

Emily opened her hands. It was tails. "Again."

"Tails."

It landed heads.

"Shit," said Kaley. "That's not good."

Emily thought about it for a moment. "No… It's good. It means your luck is normal. You're not lucky or unlucky."

"Heads."

She flipped the coin again, and it landed heads. "Sometimes you're lucky, sometimes not. I think you're okay."

"Okay. Now you."

Emily flipped the coin and called heads. It was tails. She flipped it again and called tails. It was heads. Three more flips and three more wrong guesses. "I'm still marked. Lucky me."

"I don't want you to die, Ems. I can't be the only one to survive. If I don't have you to talk to about all this, I'll lose my mind."

Emily reached out and held her hand. "I'm here."

"But how do we make sure that doesn't change?"

"I don't know, babes, but I've thought of an idea."

Kaley looked at her questioningly. "Another one?"

"Yeah, I know a guy. A guy who might like a kiss. The only

problem is that it's a bit of a walk, and there's a chance I might die getting there."

"You better hope that clover does its job then. Where is it you want to go?"

"Benford Meadows. The bad neighbourhood."

Kaley pulled a face. "The worst neighbourhood! People get mugged there all the time. And worse."

"It's the worse that I'm counting on. I would go on my own, but I need you to watch my back and try to keep my luck from catching up with me."

"I wouldn't let you go alone. You're too delicate."

"No." She shook her head. "Not any more. My days of being a pushover are finished."

Kaley squinted at her, studying her. "You mean it, don't you? You've changed."

She pulled her jumper up around her chin and realised she could smell Dante on it. It felt like an age ago her lips had been on his. "It's long overdue. Two nights ago, I didn't have a life worth saving, but now I realise how precious every day is. Also, demons are real. I mean, what the actual fuck!"

"Yeah, I guess that does change a person's perspective, huh? Also means there's a God though, which is pretty cool."

"Didn't you believe in him already?"

Kaley shrugged. "I dunno. Last few years, I've mostly zoned out whenever I've gone to the gurdwara. I'll be paying more attention from now on, though, believe me."

Emily stood up and brushed the dirt off her legs. "You ready?"

Kaley let out a massive yawn, and then she nodded. "Yeah, I'm feeling lucky."

"Well, at least that makes one of us."

CHAPTER
EIGHTEEN

EMILY TRIPPED TWICE during the hour-long walk. It was just a normal part of life now. Her foot would strike a hidden rock or slide on a discarded, rotting apple, and she would hit the deck. She was pretty sure she broke her pinkie finger on the last fall; the pain was constant and nagging, but also meaningless if she didn't remove the curse.

Kaley's presence turned out to be necessary. At one point, she may well have saved Emily's life when she had stood in the way and covered Emily when a truck hurtled by with a rear bay full of rattling metal pipes. It looked for sure like one might fly loose, but Kaley made sure that it would never have a route to Emily. So Klanek backed off and waited.

Benford Meadows was less frightening during the day, but more depressing. Garden fences sagged with disrepair and rubbish hung off bushes like filthy Christmas decorations. Graffiti covered every unprotected brick or concrete slab.

"It's well grotty around here," said Kaley as they walked past an overflowing litter bin. "How does the council let it get this bad?"

Emily held her breath to avoid smelling the doggy doodoo. It was only once they made it back into fresh air that she answered. "I assume the graffiti would be back the moment they painted over it. Kids probably get bored with nothing to do and no money to go anywhere."

"Makes you think about how much of a difference upbringing makes. One person is born with rich parents and gets a private education; another is born here to a single mum with a drug habit. Neither kid did anything to deserve it."

"Well, that's why you're becoming a solicitor, right? To make a difference. Maybe you should focus on tackling poverty."

"I think I would like that."

They carried on to the end of the path, where Emily shuddered when she realised they were near where Dante had died. Were the police in the area, or had Dante been seen as just another junkie to be shipped off to the morgue without interest?

"Do you know where we're going, Ems? I've never been here before."

"Yeah, it's this way."

They headed over the short tunnel with the overturned trolley inside and came onto the street where Samaan lived. Emily expected to see a fire engine, but there wasn't one. Instead, several metres of yellow caution tape now surrounded the blackened husk of Samaan's house, while two men stood inside the cordon, kicking at debris and marking things off on a clipboard. The fire was out, but they probably had to ensure it wouldn't collapse on top of anybody.

"That's where Samaan lived," she told Kaley. "He was inside when it went up in flames."

"Jesus. Was he trapped?"

"No. It's a long story, but he chose to remain inside. Maybe he wanted to atone." She didn't have the energy to explain about his sister's corpse returning from the dead or the cat-skull altars in his living room. "I need to keep my head down," she said. "Some of the neighbours saw me leaving with Dante earlier and I haven't changed my clothes."

"What happened to Dante? You said he overdosed."

"A junkie stabbed him with a needle."

Kaley recoiled. "That's horrible. Needles freak me out so much. I still can't believe I got a tattoo."

"I thought you were brave," said Emily. "Come on, this way."

They walked along the pavement for a minute, and then Emily stopped them at the end of a garden path. A pebble-dashed grey house stood at the end of it, ugly in every way.

"You might want to stay here, Kay, because a junkie lives here. Last night, he threatened to rape me."

"Fucking hell, Emily. What are we doing here?"

"What do you think? Can you think of someone better to kiss?"

"You're going to kiss him?"

"Damn right I am." She marched up the uneven path and knocked on the door. No one answered, so she knocked three more times until a chain rattled and someone yanked the door open with a stiff judder.

The same junkie from last night appeared in the doorway. He was wearing stained boxer shorts and nothing else, exposing a full complement of ribs. He didn't seem happy to see her. "Yeah? What the fuck do you want? I'm tryna kip."

He didn't recognise her. He'd been so high last night that this was the first time he was seeing her. *What do I say? I can't just kiss him.* "Um, I heard you might… um, have some weed to sell."

"Who told ya that?"

"Samaan." *Shit, why did I pick him?*

The junkie frowned as if she'd just farted. "Samaan's dead." He nodded down the street to the burnt-out house. "Burned in a fire last night."

And I was there. You saw me you, you deadbeat.

Don't judge. Wait, I plan on killing this guy, right?

"You're kidding?" she said. "He's dead?" Once again, she surprised herself by her ability to lie. "Are you sure?"

"Yeah, I'm sure. There's been fucking anarchy around here all morning. Police, fire engines, ambulances." He spat on his own hallway wall in disgust. "Anyway, that guy was never into drugs. He kicked off about it all the time, like he thought he was better than the rest of us. Weird character he was. Glad he's gone."

Very neighbourly of you. "Yeah, I didn't like him either. I guess he must have lied to me then to mess with me. Just thought you might be willing to sell me some," she shrugged, "and maybe chill out for a bit."

He raised an eyebrow. "You want to hang?"

Emily looked back at Kaley, who did not look at all comfortable. Then she saw a woman across the street watching with interest. *Does she recognise me from last night? Shit, I need to hurry this up.* "Yeah, sure. If you're all right with that. I got no place to be."

He chuckled. "Looks like you've already partied enough. You been doing blow or summin'?"

"I'm just tired. That's why I want some weed. It helps me sleep."

He nodded. "Me too. Look, I ain't really a dealer, but I can spare a bit if you want to pay me over the odds for it – say twenty per cent. I can restock later from my guy then."

She nodded. "That's cool. Thanks, I appreciate it."

"Your friend coming in, too?"

"Yeah, but she's not into weed. It's against her religion."

He rolled his eyes. "Just like Samaan. She Syrian too."

"I'm English," said Kaley from the bottom of the path. "I don't mind chilling while you two smoke."

Emily nodded to assure him. "She's easy-going."

He seemed to think for a moment, but then he shoved open the door and stood to the side. "Then come on in, ladies. Excuse the mess."

Emily shuddered as she brushed past him and entered the hallway. He stunk of BO and alcohol. His flat stunk of marijuana, and a microwave curry that had been left on the kitchen counter cooked but uneaten. Disgustingly, it actually made her tummy rumble. She hadn't slept or eaten in far too long.

The junkie led them into a living room that was surprisingly neat. There was a scratched leather couch that still had most of its shape, and a decent-sized television with a SKY box underneath it. *Bargain Hunt* was playing.

He watches Bargain Hunt? *Takes all kinds, I guess.*

"Take a seat," he said, almost proudly. "Want a cuppa? I've got crisps, if you're hungry?"

"Yeah," said Kaley. "I'm starving. Thanks."

He smiled. "Coming right up."

Once he padded barefoot into the kitchen, Kaley sat down on the couch and put her hands on her knees. She looked at Emily curiously. "This guy threatened to rape you? I reckon you could snap him like a twig."

"Yeah, well, he's sober now. Last night, he was a piece of shit, and he killed Dante."

Kaley grunted. "Drugs. This all started with drugs. If we hadn't popped pills with Harry, none of this would have happened."

Emily sat down beside her and rubbed at her eyes. "We should have listened to our parents, huh? Don't do drugs. Yeah, no shit."

The sound of a kettle boiling came from the kitchen, and the junkie began to whistle the tune to *EastEnders*. Emily called out to him. "Um, what was your name, by the way?"

"Steve. What's yours?"

"Gemma. Gemma and…"

"Sharna," said Kaley, and then she shrugged at Emily with a bemused look on her face. "It was the first thing that came to me."

"It's pretty." Emily looked around the room while she waited for Steve to return. She saw various photographs on the wall of a younger, healthier man. In the largest of the pictures, he was standing next to a young girl with his arm around her waist and a bright smile on his face. Other pictures had him standing with two older people who must have been his parents. He didn't look so happy in those.

Steve re-entered the room with two mugs of tea and a pack of crisps in his teeth. He set the mugs down on the carpet, which had several ring stains already. Then he tossed the crisps to Kaley, who ripped them open greedily. When she tasted them, however, she groaned. "Prawn cocktail? Seriously?"

He actually blushed. "They're my favourite. I'm weird. So, um, where you girls from? Not from around here."

"I live at Gosforth Court," said Emily, which was the truth.

"Finchley," said Kaley.

He whistled. "You're a Fincher? It's right posh around there. I used to dream of living in one of them big houses at the end of the main drag."

"I don't live in the mansions," said Kaley. "I live in one of the houses on Foxglove Avenue."

He nodded. "Still… you're lucky."

Emily and Kaley flinched at the word.

"Thanks," said Kaley. "Did you grow up around here, Steve?"

"No." He rubbed at his bare arms and gave a little shiver. "My family live up in Burnley. I came down here to live with a couple of mates when I was younger. Thought it would be a laugh. The two of them left eventually, but I'm still here."

"It's nice," said Kaley, looking around and smiling thinly.

"You taking the piss? This place is a shithole. You don't have to be polite."

Kaley cleared her throat. "I just meant you obviously try to keep it neat."

"What happened to you, Steve?" Emily studied him and wondered how he was still breathing. His cheekbones looked like they were about to erupt from his skin, as did his ribs, and his eyes were sunk deeply into his skull. "It seems like you come from a nice family based on the pictures on the wall. How did you end up like this?"

Kaley tutted. "Way to judge, Ems."

He frowned. "Ems?"

"Just a nickname."

"Oh, right."

Rather than take offence from her enquiry, Steve seemed embarrassed. "You came here to buy drugs. You ain't perfect, are ya?"

"No, I'm not. But, honestly, I'm interested in your story. Tell me what happened."

"Not much to tell. My dad used to beat me and my sister around a bunch, which was a living hell. Then, when I was twelve, I got diagnosed as having behavioural problems and was expelled from school. Nowadays I know I'm bipolar, but back then no one cared." He shrugged. "They don't care much now either. The last straw was when I were sixteen and my sis were fourteen. Our neighbour was a good friend of our dad, and he used to come round all the time. One night, he came round and abused my sister. Dad didn't believe her, so he beat the shit out of her for lying. I left home a week after that."

Kaley groaned. "You left her."

"Yeah. My plan was to get set up and then have her come live with me, but… I got into drugs and the rest is history. I think it were the guilt of leaving her in that place by herself that sent me on a spiral. It got so intense that I just needed to shut it all off, you know? Now I can't remember the last night I didn't get high."

"Do you ever see your sister?" Emily asked.

"No. Not no more." He left it at that. "Anyway, you came here to chill. Let me go grab a joint." He wandered off again into the kitchen.

Kaley turned on the sofa to face Emily. Despite not liking prawn cocktail, she had finished off the bag. "What a train wreck. He likes you, though, I can tell. Are you gonna kiss him already so we can get the fuck out of here?"

"I'm working up to it. Maybe once he's had some weed. I... I need a little time to— Shit!" She knocked her tea over with her foot. Her bad luck was still in play.

Steve came racing back into the room with a joint between his bony fingers. "Everything okay?"

"I'm so sorry, I spilled tea everywhere."

"What? Oh, don't worry about it. Accidents happen, don't they?"

Emily nodded and smiled, but she couldn't hold it in any longer. "You threatened to rape me last night, and you killed my friend Dante."

He actually staggered as though she'd punched him. "What? Are you crazy?"

"No, I'm not. I'm tired and upset and close to crazy, but I'm not there yet. You and me met last night. Don't you remember?"

"I..." His mouth fell open, but he only seemed confused.

Steve staggered again, almost dropping his unlit joint. "I... I thought you looked familiar, but I couldn't see how I would know a girl like you."

"Forget that," said Emily. "How about the fact you threatened to rape me? Do you remember or not?"

"No, I don't. Sorry..." He slumped against the wall. "I were out me tree last night. I did a load of H. Usually I only smoke a bit of weed, but a mate had some to share. Look, if I hurt you last night, I didn't mean it."

"You didn't hurt me," she spat. "But you did hurt my friend Dante when you stabbed him with a needle and injected him. He overdosed."

"What? No..."

"Yes!"

"No, that kid is fine. He was here earlier, snooping around Samaan's place."

Emily growled, annoyed by his attempt to confuse her. "The hell are you talking about? He's dead."

"He ain't. Syrian kid, yeah? I seen him around a few times before with Samaan. He was in a bit of a state this morning, but he was breathing. Stood watching the firemen put out the flames, he was, like he wanted to make sure Samaan was really dead or summin'. Gave me a right horrible look when he seen me. Makes sense now that you're here. I really stabbed him with a needle?"

Emily nodded. "Yeah, you did. He got really high and then he… died."

"He must have just passed out. Believe me, after a hit of good H you can leave your body. Once I fell asleep against a radiator. Burned the shit out of my back and I never even woke up."

"Are you telling me the truth? Is Dante really alive?"

Steve looked at the joint in his fingers and tucked it behind his ear. He looked even more tired than she was. "Maybe I was hallucinating, but I swear I saw him this morning. I'm not lying to you. And… I'm sorry for what I did. I would never hurt someone intentionally."

"You mean you wouldn't sober," said Kaley. "But it's still your fault if you hurt someone when you're drunk or high."

Emily nodded. "You make the choice to get that way."

"I'm a piece of shit. What else do you want me to say? I steal and I mug people. I do all kinds of horrible things when I'm out me tree. Then I do drink and drugs to forget about them. It's a merry-go-round I can never get off."

"You can," said Kaley. "You can get help."

He rolled his eyes. "Yeah, okay. You think I ain't tried, love? Live my life for a while, then tell me how easy it is to change. Go back to your nice little lives, yeah, and let me live mine. I don't even know what you're doing here. It ain't to get high, is it? You should go."

Kaley gave Emily a look. Their plan had gone to shit. *Because I couldn't keep a lid on my anger.*

"I came here to kill you," she said. "Believe it or not."

His mouth fell open. "W-What?"

She shook her head. "Never mind. Now that I'm here, I can't do it. You *are* a piece of shit, Steve, but you also didn't ask to grow up in a house where you and your sister weren't safe. Seems like some people are just born unlucky, and it would be wrong for me to punish you when I don't know what it's like to be you."

"You couldn't kill me. You're just a girl."

She chuckled. "I reckon I outweigh you by at least a couple of stone, Steve, so I think I could give it an excellent shot. But I wasn't planning to fight you, anyway. My plan was something a lot more subtle. It doesn't matter now, though, because I forgive you for last night. I don't trust that you won't hurt someone again in the future, but I don't want to carry the anger with me, so I'll forgive you and let it go."

Steve stared down at the carpet. "All right. Thanks then. I really am sorry."

"I believe you. You're not evil, you're just weak. I get it. Sometimes it's easier to let life drag you along than to take control. Right now, I need you to help me."

He nodded. "Yeah, okay. What do you need?"

"I need to find Dante. You live around here. Do you know where he lives?"

"Not exactly, but I know where the Syrian boys hang about during the day. Most of 'em work nights during the week, so they chill out together in the afternoons sometimes."

Emily stood up. "Take me there."

"I'll get some clothes on." He wandered off into the hallway.

Kaley stood up next to Emily. "Guess nobody's getting kissed then?"

"There's still time. First, I want to see if he's telling the truth about Dante. If he's lying, then I'm gonna plant the biggest smacker on him he's ever had."

"We'll call this plan B then. You really think there's a chance Dante didn't die last night?"

"I don't know," she admitted. "But I pray he's okay."

Kaley smirked and elbowed her in the ribs. "Girl, you've got a thing for the lad, ain't ya? Maybe that's the reason you're refusing to let this curse kill you. Gotta get ya sex on."

"Shut up you!"

Steve came back into the room wearing a orange puffer jacket with a button-up shirt underneath. He completed the ensemble with tracksuit bottoms and dress shoes. "Curse?" he said, frowning. "Who's cursed?"

"We all are," said Emily. "The whole of humankind."

He raised an eyebrow. "Yeah, I hear that. Okay, let's go."

Emily followed the junkie out of the room, undecided whether or not to kiss him. She would decide soon.

Is Dante still alive?

CHAPTER
NINETEEN

EMILY AND KALEY linked arms as they walked through the dense housing estate. Suspicious stares met them on every street, and based on their pyjamas and dressing gowns, many of the residents didn't have jobs. It was almost noon.

"Just 'round here," said Steve, pointing ahead. "I think that Dante kid lives in one of the flats down Cartwright Close."

That meant nothing to Emily so she simply nodded. She'd lived her entire life in Boole, but never before had she set foot around these parts. It was rough – even rougher than where Samaan had lived. Wheelie bins were knocked over, spilling rubbish onto the roads, lamppost covers were missing, and one house had a grime-caked washing machine dumped in its muddy front garden.

Kaley grabbed Emily and moved her aside forcefully. She yelped, but then realised a teenager on a bicycle was racing out of an alleyway and about to hit her. The front tyre missed her leg by two inches.

Steve hollered after the kid. "Watch where you're going, dickhead!"

"Fuck off!" he yelled back. From the look of him, he should've been at school.

Steve shook his head and grunted. "Bloody kids."

"Are we almost there?" asked Emily. She was trembling at the prospect of seeing Dante alive. If he was alive, then she had abandoned him on that bench when he had needed her help.

"Right," said Steve. "It's proper dodgy 'round here, so don't cause any aggro."

Kaley frowned. "Why would we cause aggro?"

"Didn't you come to my gaff to kill me? Seems like you two are pretty good at finding trouble."

Emily chuckled and raised her eyebrow at Kaley. "He has a point."

"Yeah, I suppose he does."

Steve led them down another couple of roads. Truanting teenagers hung around with ill intent, sitting on brick walls or loitering inside cars. People watched suspiciously from their windows, a tapestry of skin colours including plenty of dour-looking white people. This was Boole's skid row, and all were welcome so long as you were poor.

And Dante lives here? He doesn't deserve to be in a place like this. No one does.

Steve took them to a small two-storey block of flats with whitewashed walls that were crumbling in several places. On the corner, a satellite dish hung at a precarious angle, gravity trying to yank it free.

"This is where a lot of the Syrian boys hang out. Inside, on the stairwell."

Emily nodded. "Show me."

"I'm off, love. I brought you here, so now you don't need me."

"Wrong. We might need help getting out of here, so you need to stick with us."

Kaley put a hand on the arm of his orange puffer jacket. Somewhere inside must have been his bony wrist. "You wouldn't leave a couple of defenceless girls on their own, would you?"

He tipped his head back and groaned. "Just make it quick. My head's banging and I want to go to bed."

"Join the club," said Emily.

Steve went over and jabbed a button on the intercom. There was an answer almost immediately. "'ello?"

"Hiya, can you let us in, please? We're looking for... um, Dante, yeah?"

The person didn't reply, but there was an electronic chirp and the door thudded. Steve shoved it and held it open.

Emily frowned. "Did you even know that person?"

"Nah, but they don't care who I am, do they?"

The interior hallway was grim. The floor was dark concrete with a sheen that might have been piss, or possibly spilled alcohol. There was a pile of fag butts in the corner near the stairs, and the window on the back wall had metal security bars over it. There were only four doors, each a featureless wooden slab painted red with old-fashioned brass letter boxes. "Which one is Dante's flat?"

Steve shrugged. "No idea, love. Just knock on a door and ask, innit?"

"Really? Just a random person's door?"

"They're just people. Be respectful and they won't stab you."

Emily realised he was being sarcastic, but also that she was being judgemental. If she were in a nice part of town, she wouldn't fear knocking on a stranger's door to ask for help.

"Okay." She moved up to the first door on her left and rapped it with her knuckles.

No one answered.

So she tried the next door. This time she had better luck. A woman opened the door but kept it on the chain. She peered at Emily through the slender gap. "Yes? Can I help you?"

Emily smiled. "Sorry to bother you. I'm looking for a friend of mine. Dante?"

The eyes in the gap narrowed. "You know Dante?"

"I met him recently down at the pier. He told me he lived here, but I've forgotten his flat number."

The woman didn't answer, just kept staring.

Emily cleared her throat. "I know you have no reason to trust me, but I swear he's my friend. I really need to talk to him."

"Flat six. Upstairs."

"Thank you. Thank you so m—"

The woman closed the door.

Emily turned to the staircase. "Guess we're going up."

They ascended the steps, which were the same as the floor – slippery concrete. On the top landing, they encountered a man talking to another in an open doorway. When they saw Emily, they went inside. Fortunately, not into flat six.

Are you alive, Dante?

She paused in front of the door with a brass number six on it. Kaley moved up beside her and touched her hand. "You okay?" she asked.

"I don't even know what's real any more. Dante was dead. I saw him with my own eyes."

"Well, let's find out for sure." Kaley knocked on the door.

No one answered.

She knocked again.

No one answered.

Emily turned to Steve and scowled. "I told you! He's... He's not here."

He backed off. "I swear it was him. Black T-shirt, long-sleeved, yeah?"

"He wore that last night. Do you think... Do you think, maybe, that you're remembering last night when you were high?"

Steve put a hand to his head and winced. "Shit, I don't know. Maybe. Like I said, I took some pretty heavy shit."

"You killed him," said Emily, more resigned than angry. "Just like I thought. You shot him full of junk and killed him."

"I'm sorry."

"Stop saying that!"

Kaley huffed and banged on the door again. Then she tried the handle. It was unlocked.

"Hey, what are you doing?" Emily frowned. "You can't just—"

Kaley pushed the door open and stepped into the hallway. "I'm just looking. Where's the harm?"

Emily groaned and went in after her. It wasn't right to go through a dead man's home, but that was what she was seemingly doing.

The hallway was painted a light brown. The radiator on the wall was rusted and hanging askew. Underfoot, cheap lino peeled at the edges. A kitchen lay directly ahead, a lounge on the left.

Emily went inside the lounge and Kaley followed. They gasped at what they saw.

"No." Emily shook her head. "No, I don't understand."

In the centre of the room, stacked on top of a coffee table, was a series of browning cat skulls. The same cross symbols she'd seen in Samaan's house had been painted on all four walls in crude red paint. Or blood.

Kaley scrunched up her nose. "What the hell is this?"

"A shrine," Emily muttered. "To Klanek."

Steve grunted. "Who the hell is Klanek?"

"A bad guy."

"I think we should get the hell out of here then. These Syrians are into some weird shit."

Emily shook her head. It made no sense. If Dante worshipped Klanek, then why did he fight Samaan? Had it all been a lie? Was she being played somehow?

I trusted him.

She tugged at the jumper he had given her and suddenly felt itchy, so she yanked it over her head and tossed it onto the carpet. "He lied to me."

Kaley eyed the cat skulls, fidgeting with the buttons on her coat. "It's not your fault, Ems. Men lie."

"But he was so kind to me. All he wanted was to put a stop to all of this."

"All of what?" Steve was standing in the doorway, glancing around furtively. "This is weird."

Emily let out a sigh. "It's nothing."

Feeling suddenly unwell, and realising she was most probably going to die soon, she barged her way past Steve and Kaley and went back out onto the landing. She lurched over the banister and vomited. Her stomach was empty, so it was little more than drool.

Kaley rushed straight out to rub her back.

"I'm going to die," she moaned.

"No. No, you're not, babes. I won't let you."

Steve came out behind them and folded his arms, awkward, and confused, and more than a little worse for wear.

"I've already survived longer than I should have." She reached into her jeans pocket and pulled out the clover. It was falling apart now. She let it go over the banister and watched it flutter down towards the pissy concrete below.

"Don't give up," Kaley leaned in and whispered. "What about plan A? Kiss Steve."

Emily groaned. The clover was still fluttering, as though it were desperate not to touch the dirty floor.

A black cat peered up at her.

"You!"

Kaley stepped out of Emily's way with a yelp as she rushed away from the railing and hurtled down the stairs. "Where are you going?"

Emily leapt off the bottom steps and landed on the concrete. Her weak ankle rolled, and she cried out in pain, but she refused to fall down. She turned to where she'd seen the cat.

But it was gone.

Dante stood in the entryway to the flats. When he saw her, he froze. "E-Emily? What are you doing here?"

He looked like shit, his skin pale and sweaty, his eyes bloodshot and watery. But he was alive.

"Dante? You're okay?"

"I've been better, but yes."

"I thought you were dead."

He opened his mouth to speak, but movement on the stairs caught his attention as Steve moved up beside Emily and pointed a finger at Dante. "I told you! Ha! He's alive, see!"

"No thanks to you," said Dante, glaring.

"Oh, yeah. Look, mate, I'm really s—"

"Who are you?" Emily demanded. "Why do you have a shrine to Klanek in your living room? I want answers."

Dante nodded wearily. "I will give them to you. You deserve the truth."

"Damn right I do. And make it quick because I'm due to die soon."

"I'm hoping it won't come to that. Follow me."

Dante moved to the bottom of the stairs, but Emily didn't follow. "You need to trust me," he said.

"I *did* trust you, but you lied."

"I didn't. Come upstairs and I'll explain. You have nothing to fear."

"Yeah," said Steve. "I'll protect you."

Kaley rolled her eyes. "You couldn't protect a fly from a spider."

"Fine. I'll go home then. Don't need this stress."

"No," said Emily. "Come."

Steve might have been an emaciated druggie, but he was better than nothing. And she witnessed last night that he could put up quite a fight when provoked.

They followed Dante upstairs and went back inside his flat. When they re-entered the lounge, Emily shuddered at the sight of the cat skulls. "Are you worshipping Klanek?"

"I didn't tell you all of my past." Dante looked at the shrine for a moment, but then turned away, almost in shame. "When my parents died," he said, "I was still young. For a time, I was on the streets, begging for food. My parents' money was still in a bank and not yet given to me. Without legal help, it probably would've remained there, but a local organisation took me in and cared for me, got me back on my feet."

"The Sect of Klanek."

"Yes. When I said Samaan and I were brothers, I meant it in several ways. He and I served together until I ran away one night with an old friend. I did not wish to be a part of the sect any longer. Even in my youth, I saw the evil in it. Only Allah should decide men's fates."

"Got anything to eat, mate?" asked Steve. He was scratching at his arms through the cuffs of his jacket.

"No." Dante looked at Emily. "Why is he here? This is the man who—"

"I know who he is. It's a long story, but if not for Steve, I wouldn't even know you were still alive. How are you not dead?"

"A miracle, perhaps? I don't know. I had the strangest dreams; happy memories of my parents and childhood friends. Then I woke up and thought I was going to die. My head was imploding and my heart was beating out of my chest. I had woken up from unconsciousness, alone and confused. I didn't know what to do, so I came home to prepare."

"Prepare what? Where were you coming back from?"

He reached into his pocket and pulled out a bottle of salt. "I had to go to the shops to get this. It'll help with the ritual."

"What ritual?" asked Kaley. She was standing in the doorway, frowning like she had a headache. "What the hell is all this?"

Dante noticed his jumper on the ground. He knelt to pick it up, then looked at Emily. "I want to help you. I'm going to make a bargain."

She shook her head. The cat skulls kept creeping into the edge of her vision and making her shudder. "What bargain? What are you talking about? I'm fed up with this. Occult symbols, demon cults, and black cats... It's all insane."

He flinched. "Black cats? What do you mean?"

"I mean, there's a frikkin' black cat I keep seeing everywhere. I think... I think it's been trying to help me."

Dante groaned. "No. That cat is not trying to help you. It is an aspect of Klanek. If you've been seeing a cat – if it's been offering you aid – then Klanek wishes for you to live."

"What? You're saying the cat is Klanek, and that he's trying to kill me and help me at the same time?"

"He's bound by the contract Samaan made, but there's a way he can break it. If you pledge yourself to him, then you'll gain his protection. He's shown an interest in you, Emily. He wants you in his service."

Kaley rolled her eyes. "All the guys want you this week, don't they?"

Emily grunted. "Maybe Lily had the right idea. Girls are less hassle."

"Debatable, but at least they don't try to kill you so often."

"So..." she narrowed her eyes at Dante, thinking, "if I serve Klanek, can he bring my friends back?"

"No. His powers are not so unbridled. I don't know what bargain Samaan made to bring back his sister, but it's beyond my knowledge. If you serve Klanek, you'll be required to decide the fates of men. You will have to kill at his whim in exchange for great riches, knowledge, and power. Most who serve him in the sect are not bound to Him so closely. It is a dangerous, lifelong commitment. Only those who serve at the very top offer themselves completely."

"And that's what you're planning to do?" asked Emily.

He turned the salt bottle and emptied some onto the cat-skull altar. "In exchange for your safety."

She frowned, and her eyes drifted towards the walls and the

occult symbols painted on them. Was he telling the truth? Had he really gone to buy table salt to help with a ritual to bind himself to the whims of a demon? For her?

"Why would you do this for me?"

He was clearly exhausted, but he stood firm as he looked her in the eye. "Because I have things to make right, and whatever evil I might do in service of Klanek will be offset by the good you will do."

"What good? I work at a shop."

"I see you, Emily. There's a great goodness in you. Your soul is worth more than mine. Perhaps in saving it I can please Allah and be forgiven for my sins."

"By serving a demon?" said Kaley. "I doubt it."

Steve cleared his throat. "Can I just ask, what the fuck are you people going on about? Am I high? Are you high? Seriously, somebody has to be high right now."

Kaley grabbed his arm. "Just stand there and be quiet. We're figuring things out."

"Yeah, okay. I'll... I'll just stand here."

"I can't let you sign your life away to help me," said Emily, shaking her head at Dante. "I won't let you."

"Which is why you're worth doing this for. My mind's made up. I'm going to do this." He shrugged. "It's not all bad. I'll be rich and powerful too."

"Do you want that?"

"No."

"Then don't be so stupid."

Kaley cleared her throat. "How does the ritual work?"

"It's almost complete," said Dante. "The shrine has been primed with ancient words spoken. The room is enclosed with Klanek's emblem and he is bound to the earth with salt. I have added the skulls of animals sacrificed in the proper way."

Steve grunted. "Did you just have those sitting around in a cupboard or something?"

"No," said Dante, but then he added, "in a box under my

bed. I brought them with me from Syria. I think I always knew Klanek would regain my service one day."

"So what else is left to do?" asked Kaley.

Emily shushed her. "It doesn't matter because he's not doing it."

Dante pulled out a knife from inside his belt. It had a dark blade, like the one Samaan had possessed. "Iron," he explained. "All that's left is the spilling of blood upon the altar."

"You mean your coffee table," said Steve. "Very holy."

"Will you be quiet," said Dante. "Or leave my home."

Emily gave Steve a chiding look. "Stop speaking."

She then moved up to Dante and slowly took his wrist. She looked him in the eyes. "I won't let you do this for me. I've lost half of the people I care about, but I won't let you throw your life away. How could I live with that?"

"Please, Emily."

"You're not doing it."

She moved her hand down his wrist and took the knife, placing it on the coffee table beside the cat skulls. "If I'm going to die today, then I want to spend it with you." She reached out and took his hands in hers. "Let's just… go get a coffee. I want to sit and talk and learn everything I can about you. There are worse ways to go. This time tomorrow, I'll probably be sipping cappuccino with Jesus."

"Fuck that, babes!"

Emily turned around, surprised by Kaley's fierce tone.

What she saw surprised her even more.

Kaley had grabbed the dark-bladed knife in her right hand and was holding up her left. She sliced into her palm so deeply that blood spurted everywhere. It went all over the cat skulls, painting them red.

Dante yelled out in horror. "What have you done?"

Kaley was smiling. "I'm saving my friend's life. Time to speak to the manager."

"Kaley? What have you done?" Emily couldn't believe what

she was seeing. Her friend was bleeding all over the place, and in obvious pain, but she was smiling.

Steve was squealing in horror. He ran to the corner of the room and covered his face. "Tell me when it stops bleeding. I… I'm gonna be sick."

"No," Dante shouted. "No, no, no."

Kaley continued leaking blood onto the skulls, grinning like a maniac. "What now? How do I know if it's worked?"

"What are you doing?" Emily shook her head. "Why?"

"Erm, great power, knowledge, riches. I'm happy to take that on if it means I can save you, Ems."

"I don't want that. I don't want anyone to suffer for me."

"I want to do good in the world, Ems. This is how I can do it. Superpowers, just like I dreamed of as a kid."

"You're a fool," said Dante. "A fool."

"Ah, don't be such a hypocrite. A young guy like you can make a deal with a demon, but not a brown-faced girl?"

"It isn't like that. Klanek cares nothing about good or bad, only about the souls he can corrupt to his will. He serves the Adversary."

She shrugged. "And I serve me. If Klanek's got any sense, he'll negotiate mutually agreeable terms. When I tell him what I —" Her words choked and she went stiff as a board. Her jaws locked together. She let out a guttural moan.

Emily turned to Dante and saw the panic in his eyes. "What's happening to her? What's wrong?"

He shook his head and sighed. "The ritual was accepted."

"What does that mean?"

Before he answered, Kaley's body loosened, and she regained control over herself. Her smile returned to her face. "Oh, Emily, I've done it. You're safe. Klanek has granted me my wish and removed your mark."

Dante was shaking his head.

Emily was doing the same. "What are you talking about?"

"Call it a signing bonus," said Kaley. "In exchange for my oath, Klanek granted me a wish. You're safe, Ems. We did it."

"But at what cost?" Dante moaned. "You don't understand what you've done."

"I understand everything." She spoke dreamily, her eyes almost looking right through them. "Klanek is with me. I feel his love, his warmth, his protection. You're wrong about him, Dante. He wants only good for those who worship him. Men like Samaan abuse His power, but I won't do that. I asked Him to save Emily's life and he said yes. He is good."

Emily shook her head. Kaley sounded like she was high, her voice airy and euphoric. "Kay, I'm worried. You're scaring me."

"Don't be worried, Ems. I've saved you, but there's someone else who still needs my help."

"Who?"

"The poor barmaid that Harry kissed." She threw an arm towards the wall and, impossibly, a circle of light spread across the peeling wallpaper. It was like watching a movie, but Emily knew she was looking at something happening right now. Like a god, she was watching the life of an unaware mortal.

The barmaid was still at work, gathering something from a stockroom filled with crates of beer and alcopops. There was a large shelving unit behind her, and stacked on top of it was a big red plastic crate full of bottles. As if pushed by invisible hands, the box was slowly shifting towards the edge of the shelf. It was going to fall right on top of her head. To make matters worse, she had stopped what she was doing in order to stoop down and tie up her shoelace.

Steve gasped. "What is this?"

"An innocent victim," said Kaley. "But I'm going to save her."

The box was right on the edge of the shelf, nearly at the limit of what gravity would tolerate.

"What are you doing?" Emily asked. "Kay, what is this?"

"It's fucked up," said Steve. "She's a bloody witch. I'm off."

Steve moved away from the corner of the room and dashed for the door.

Kaley turned and slashed the iron blade through the air. It didn't stop him, and he continued right on over to the doorway, but then he staggered against the frame and bounced back into the room. One of his hands rose to his neck.

Blood spilled between his fingers.

"Am… Am I okay?" he asked, his face turning white.

Emily gasped, her hands going to her mouth. "Kaley, what the fuck? What the fuck?"

Steve toppled over and crashed right on top of the cat-skull altar and collapsed the coffee table underneath. Dante hopped back, moaning.

Kaley examined the blade. It'd already been stained with her blood, but now she had added Steve's to it. There was a glassy look in her eyes, like she was a mannequin rather than a human.

Emily stared at Steve's unmoving body. "You… killed him."

Kaley shrugged. "I killed a junkie. One who threatened to rape you and who nearly killed Dante. The world is a better place without him, and look…" She nodded at the wall, which was still shining a spotlight upon the barmaid. She had finished tying her shoelace and stood up. The precariously balanced crate shifted back onto the shelf, and she left the stockroom without ever knowing how close she had come to having an awful accident.

"She's safe?" asked Emily. "Because of what you've done?" She looked down at Steve and tried to make sense of it. If there had been a choice between a junkie with no future and a young girl with her whole life ahead of her, was Kaley right to have done what she just did?

It isn't a simple choice to make. To actually wield the knife and act so decisively. This isn't my friend. She would never hurt anyone.

"Kaley, you're not in control of yourself."

"Klanek is inside her," said Dante, and he took a step forward.

Kaley pointed the knife at him. "I saved two innocent women from a situation caused by selfish men. Samaan started this, but I just ended it. Well, almost…"

"Almost? What does that mean, Kay? Do you understand what you've done? You killed someone?"

She shook her head. "People kill every day, in war and politics, on the streets for nothing more than an insult. At least my actions will bring positive change. If the world was free of human waste like Steve, then we'd all be better off."

"Kay! This isn't you. Some people barely get given a chance in life. I thought you wanted to help them."

"I'll help those who deserve it."

Dante sneered. "And who decides that? You?"

"Yes, me." She pointed the knife at him again. "So you better be careful."

Emily moved to embrace her friend, but to her astonishment, Kaley waved the knife at her too. She stepped back and put her hands up. "Please."

Dante growled. "She is corrupted. Klanek guides her hand now."

Kaley snickered and walked backwards towards the door. "Klanek has empowered me, that's all; something no one else has ever tried to do. I won't waste the opportunities in front of me. I will punish the wicked and those who abuse their power."

Emily reached out to her again, but she was once again warned off by the knife.

Kaley paused in the doorway. "I love you, Ems. Soon, you'll see all the good I can do and you'll see that I'm right. This is just the start."

She swooped into the hallway and raced out of sight. Dante went to go after her, but Emily grabbed his arm and stopped him. "No, we can't go after her. Not yet."

She was referring to Steve. They couldn't just leave a dead

body in Dante's flat. He seemed to realise it too. "They will think I did this."

"He's bleeding all over your floor. We need to get this place cleaned up."

"There's no time," he said, looking towards the door. "We should go after Kaley."

"And what if someone finds Steve while we're gone?"

"They won't. I'll deal with him later."

"Deal with him how?"

Dante leant back against the wall and sighed. "I have experience. Back in Syria, when I first joined the sect, I was obligated to obey orders. For several years, I was an apprentice in the shadows."

"The shadows?"

"A group of assassins. Three men died by my hand. I did not know them, nor if they deserved it, but I murdered them because I was told to."

Emily put her head in her hands and tried to focus through her brain fog. "This is too much. Last week, my life was boring. Now the guy I'm crushing on tells me he's a serial killer."

"An assassin, and… wait, you're crushing on me?"

She looked at him and blinked. "Not really the important issue here."

"No, you're right." He stepped up to her and took both her hands. For some reason, she didn't flinch. He didn't scare her. Whenever his brown eyes focused on her, she felt safe. "I came here to escape my past," he said. "I waited for Allah to show me a way to atone. You are it, I am sure."

"No, I'm just a random girl who got caught in the middle of a load of masculine bullshit. If not for Samaan and Harry…" She shook her head.

"What is it?"

"Kaley hinted she had unfinished business. It's Harry. I think she's going to hurt him."

Dante nodded. "Most likely. She serves Klanek now, and far

more deeply than Samaan or I ever did. He'll demand sacrifices, and she will be eager to provide them."

Emily studied Steve's dead body and saw the truth of it. "She really is just getting started, isn't she?"

"Yes."

"Then we need to stop her. Harry is a piece of shit, but I can't let Kaley kill again. I have to save her. There needs to be a way I can get her out of this mess."

"I fear there's not."

"You also said you didn't know how Samaan brought back his sister, so I think it's safe to say you don't know everything."

He nodded. "This is true. A smart man admits he knows nothing."

She smiled. "I heard someone say something very similar recently. He told me to have faith."

"In God?"

"I think that's what he meant, but that's not what I have faith in. I have faith in Kaley. She's a good person and she's my friend. We need to break whatever hold Klanek has over her."

Dante nodded. "Then perhaps I was wrong. Perhaps she is my true chance to atone. I want to help you save your friend."

She put her arms out and hugged him. "Thank you."

"So… you're crushing on me?"

She eased back from him and rolled her eyes. "Still not the time."

"Then we should go. The sooner we save Kaley, the sooner we can discuss you and me."

"Deal."

CHAPTER
TWENTY

NOW THAT NEITHER she nor Dante was cursed, Emily was free to catch a bus. Fortunately, Dante had change, because she had lost all hers that morning.

They made it into Boole and immediately started searching for Kaley. They checked the Rock, the upper and lower beach, and even Daniel's church – which was closed. She could be anywhere, but if she was seeking Harry, then there was a chance she would try to meet up with him again, although he would be stupid to agree.

The town was abuzz, filled with families enjoying the sun and the beach. *Uncle Jack's* arcade opposite the leaning pier buzzed and chimed as people fed coins into its flashing machines. For most people in Boole, life was ordinary. For Emily, it was a race to save her last remaining friend's soul.

After an hour, it became clear they weren't going to find Kaley.

"She could've gone home to her parents," suggested Dante.

"No. It didn't seem like she was in the mood to rest. She was hyped up, excited to use her power."

"You're right. She will be up to something, but what?"

"Maybe she went to the garage where Harry works, but

with the mess we made of his face this morning, it's unlikely he'll be there. Not to mention he must be as tired as I am."

"He is also cursed, yes? Kaley kissed him?"

"Yeah, so maybe he's dead already."

There were still police everywhere, so they had to keep their heads down and stick to the side roads as they searched. By now, the police had obviously also discovered Lily's body, as they were combing the beach for evidence. Boole was abuzz with chatter as people discussed a double death in the town centre overnight. It was not a safe town by any means, but nor was it a place where people expected to be murdered – or crushed by road sweepers.

Emily had texted and called Kaley, but she had refused to answer. She could think of nothing else her friend would be interested in doing besides finding Harry, so she stuck with that assumption. He was the only other remaining part of this: the last loose end.

Twenty minutes later, Kaley finally replied.

Come to pier. We're still friends. XXX

Emily showed the message to Dante, who immediately became suspicious. "Why would Kaley go to the pier? It is falling down. It is not safe."

"We also checked there," said Emily. "We walked right past it. I mean, we kept our distance because of the police in the area, but… we would have seen her, right?"

"I don't know. I don't know how much power she has. If Klanek has truly blessed her, then… She might be able to do anything."

"Great. So, one of my oldest friends has become a supervillain. I'm gonna write a book when all this is done."

"Going to the pier could be a trap."

She nodded. "I know, but what else can we do? Besides, I believe she still cares about me. None of this is about hurting me. I'm kind of getting a whole man-hating vibe from her right now. Can't say I blame her."

"We go to the pier, then?"

She reached out and took his hand. "We stick together and we deal with this, but remember: I want to help her."

"I will do what I can, but if she kills again, I fear she may be lost to you."

"Then we need to prevent that from happening. Come on, we can be there in ten minutes."

They headed along the promenade at first, but then snaked around the back of the pub district to avoid the police. They came out of an alleyway directly opposite the pier.

Kaley wasn't there, only several men in shirts who seemed to be assessing the structural damage. There was now a section of scaffold erected on one side, holding up the sinking deck.

"She lied to us," said Dante. "She's not here."

Emily didn't see why that would be true. "No. She's here somewhere. Just not where everyone can see her."

"She's underneath the pier? Where all this started. But how can we get down there without being seen?"

"Maybe Kay will make sure we make it to her. She's powerful, right? Well, we have an invite to join her, so let's try."

And so they did, heading down the promenade for a stretch before hopping the wall down onto the beach. The tide was most of the way out now and it was getting on for 3PM. She'd been awake for well over twenty-four hours.

The pier was right ahead, and while there was various equipment placed on the beach, as well as a parked Land Rover, there were no people. All of the men in shirts were up top.

There was also something else. Something strange.

The underneath of the pier seemed to be cloaked in mist. It was like sea spray, but the sea was nowhere near. Somehow a cloud of vapour existed only in the space beneath the deck.

"She's here," said Emily.

Dante didn't say anything. His brow creased as he walked in silence beside her. Together, they approached the pier, and then went underneath.

Stepping into the mist was like pushing through plastic curtains at the zoo – the kind you pass to get into a butterfly exhibit. One minute, her face was being assaulted and she couldn't see, the next she was on the other side, inside a secret space unseen from outside.

Kaley stood in the middle of the wet sand, crooked wooden beams either side of her. When she saw Emily, she beamed with happiness. "You came!"

"Of course I did. I'm worried about you, Kay."

"Don't be. Everything is perfect. I'm going to pass my exams with the highest honours and go on to be the most successful barrister this country has ever seen. I'll reform the United Kingdom from the top to the bottom. Maybe I'll even run for Prime Minister."

She shook her head. "Kay, what are you talking about?"

"I've seen it all, Ems. Klanek has promised me everything. He will make sure it all happens. My dreams. All of them."

Emily looked at Dante and saw that he was choosing to remain quiet. This was between the two of them. "But what do you have to give in return, Kay? What does Klanek want from you?"

"Nothing that I'm not happy to give." She nodded her head, and all of a sudden Emily saw Harry tied to one of the metal struts that had been added in later years to support the pier. He was coming around from unconsciousness.

"H-How did you get him here?"

Kaley tilted her head curiously. "Do you know, I'm not quite sure. I just wanted him here, and that was enough to make it happen. Don't you see the power I've been given?"

"I do. I do see, Kaley, but I don't think you understand what you're doing. You can't kill people and expect everything to be all right. That's not who you are. The Kaley I know would never want to hurt people."

She snorted irritably, her eyes flashing with anger. "Let's just say I had a hell of a weekend. I'm not the same person I used to be."

"Yes, you are! You're just confused, hurting."

"Oh, for fuck's sake, Ems, grow a pair. When have you ever known me to doubt myself? That's your gig, not mine. I know exactly what I'm doing." She marched over to Harry and slapped him across the face with a force she should not have possessed. He let out a moan and then a whimper, then a confused grunt.

"K-Kaley? What are you…? Where am I? What the fuck?"

She hit him again, mashing his swollen lips. He spat blood and moaned again, but she showed no sympathy. "You're right where you deserve to be," she hissed. "You started all of this, Harry. You brought your anger and your toxic masculinity into our group. Matt is dead because of you. Lily is dead because of you. Ross is dead because of you."

"What? Fuck you, you crazy bitch. Let me go!" His eyes were wide with terror, and when he saw Emily, he begged her. "Untie me. She's lost the plot."

Emily moved to help him, but Kaley whipped out an arm.

The iron knife sliced through the air inches from her face and embedded itself in a wooden beam behind her. It was enough to stop her in her tracks, and the breath in her lungs.

"Stay back," warned Kaley. "I won't let you stop me from doing this. Harry deserves to die, and Klanek demands it. I am his servant."

"Don't do this," said Dante. "It's a path from which you can never return."

"Count yourself lucky that Emily likes you, mate, or you'd be next on my list."

Emily felt tears burning her eyes. She barely recognised her friend, but she must still be in there. If Kaley was gone, then that meant Emily had lost everyone. "Please, don't do this, Kay. Just let him go. People screw up. We let anger and fear and jealousy control us, but all of us are suffering in our own way. Harry's afraid of his father. He hasn't said so, but it's obvious, isn't it? All of the crap that comes out of his mouth has been put there by a man who is supposed to teach him right from wrong. Harry failed us because someone failed him. Give him a chance. Let him atone." She looked at Dante. "Everyone deserves a chance to leave the past behind."

Kaley had been moving towards Harry, but she stopped now, a few feet in front of him. He was wearing a button-up shirt and a pair of jeans. Obviously he'd changed since their last encounter, probably because of all the blood from his lips.

"Please," said Harry. "She's right. My dad's a fucking bully. He's constantly telling me to be a man and not to take any shit. I swear, the only time he's ever proud of me is when I come home with a black eye. The last thing I ever wanted to be was like him, but…" He shook his head, tears staining his cheeks. "I fucked up and I'm sorry."

Kaley looked him in the eye. "Truly, you're sorry? You understand what a racist piece of shit you are?"

"Yeah. Yeah, I do. I'm sorry. I want to do better."

"Well, that's a start, I guess." Kaley let out a sigh and half turned away. "Maybe there's hope for him yet."

Emily smiled, so relieved that she wanted to flop to the ground and giggle.

But then Kaley gave an animalistic grunt that sent a shiver down her spine. "But Ross has zero hope left because he's dead." She turned back to Harry. "And you need to pay for that."

Emily raced forward. "Kaley, no!"

Kaley thrust out a hand, sliding it through a gap between the buttons of Harry's shirt. She gripped his stomach, and a grin spread across her face as he began to screech. It was so loud that the men on the pier should've easily heard it, but Emily knew that for some reason they wouldn't.

Emily skidded in the sand, frozen by horror. "Stop it!"

But Kaley didn't listen. She yanked back her hand, clutching what appeared to be Harry's stomach, a slick red bag with veins all over it. Attached was a length of sinewy tubing that got longer and longer the more she pulled.

Harry's screams turned to incoherent garbles as his mouth opened wide in a silent shriek. His eyes bulged out of his head.

Kaley pulled more and more of his intestines, while crushing his stomach to pulp in her hand. At the same time, she cackled. She was enjoying this.

Emily staggered backwards.

Dante caught her. "It is too late," he moaned in her ear. "She is too far gone."

Emily nodded, knowing it was true. Kaley was lost forever.

Harry's chin fell to his chest, and bloody drool spilled from his ruined mouth. Kaley tossed his insides onto the wet sand and kicked them away. A nearby brown crab scuttled over and started shovelling sticky morsels into its mouth.

Emily wanted to throw up, but her body was empty. She slumped against Dante but managed to keep her eyes on Kaley. "Y-You're insane. You're a butcher."

Kaley smirked. "A butcher? I like that. My intention is to cleave apart the unjust systems in this country. Perhaps that's what they'll nickname me in time."

Emily found her last remaining strength and marched across the bloody sand towards her former friend. "You're a murderer! Whatever you think you're doing, you've lost your mind. Klanek is evil, and by serving him, so are you."

Kaley jolted. Her mouth opened a little, but she found no words. Instead, she shook her head sadly and turned away.

"We have to find a way to reverse what you've done," said Emily. "You can't pledge your soul to a demon. Are you serious?"

Kaley turned back around to face Emily and shrugged. "It's done. I can't reverse it even if I wanted to. So you have a choice."

"What choice?"

"You're either with me or against me."

"Kay, don't do this."

"Do what? I've made my choice, so now it's your turn. I love you, Ems, but this is happening whether you like it or not. Harry deserved to die. You know it."

"I don't believe that. He was just mixed up. He could've changed if he'd been given time."

"He had time. He wasted it." She took a step towards Emily, and it felt like being looked upon by a hungry lizard. Goosebumps erupted all over her arms. "Ems, I can give you anything. You want to win the lottery? Done! Buy your mum a mansion, never have to work again... I can give it all to you."

Emily shook her head. "In exchange for my soul? No thanks."

"No." Kaley smiled. "Not yours. His." She nodded past her, over her shoulder, towards Dante, who had remained a few metres back.

"What? What are you asking me to do?"

"Sacrifice Dante to Klanek, and he will give you whatever you wish. Just be my friend, like always, and we can have the world. Your dreams can come true, Ems. Think about it"

Emily *did* think about it. Winning the lottery. Paying back her mum's years of love with an easy life blessed with money. It would be amazing. "The problem with that, Kay, is that I don't have any dreams to make true. I've never been the ambitious type."

"You can change."

She shook her head. "No, and I don't want to. I'm pretty good with who I am. I can't let you do this."

Kaley's face broke into a monstrous sneer. "Too bad I'm not asking for your permission."

Emily went to say something, but Kaley swatted her aside like a fly. She crashed into one of the crooked wooden beams so hard it actually moved. The impact knocked the air out of her lungs and left her clawing for dear life in the sand.

Dante roared in anger and sprinted towards Kaley. He was quick enough to get the jump on her, but she was unnaturally strong. She grabbed him by the arm and swung him around until he, too, went crashing into one of the wooden beams.

The pier creaked overhead.

Emily caught her breath and got up onto her hands and knees. "Kaley, think about your family. Would they want you to do this?"

"My family wants me to be great."

"Then... what about Ross? He was kind, gentle... He would never want you to hurt anyone. He loved you."

"No, he didn't. He loved you!" She roared in anger and kicked Emily in the stomach. She crashed backwards against the unsteady beam. "You've never had to work for anything for a day in your life. Everything is easy for you. No pressure. No parents pestering you for perfect grades. No religion forcing you to be a nice girl that a fine Sikh man would wish to marry. No brown skin holding you back."

Emily groaned in pain. "I always loved you, Kay. I would've done anything for you."

"Too late."

Metal fasteners squeaked. Wet wood groaned.

The pier was about to come down on top of them.

Kaley didn't seem to realise. She marched across the sand and pulled Dante up to his feet like a rag doll. He was clutching his ribs and groaning in agony. "I am going to kill you," she threatened. "Then Emily is going to have the most amazing life ever. You want to atone, then here's your chance."

Dante gasped, but then managed to speak. "I accept. Kill me."

"N-No," said Emily. "D-Don't!"

Kaley grabbed Dante by the throat and rammed him backwards against a wooden beam. It cracked like a twig, a fissure appearing two feet above Dante's head.

Kaley screamed and threw up her arms. Dante realised a

split second later and did the same. Together they caught the broken end of the wooden beam while the opposite end crashed into the sand behind them. Their arms quivered with the exertion. If not for Kaley's newly acquired strength, they likely would have been crushed beneath it immediately. If either one of them moved, it would come down on their heads. They were trapped.

Emily clambered to her feet, clutching her burning ribs. Her swollen ankle ached and caused her to limp. What she saw before her was like a mirage – Dante and Kaley standing chest to chest with their arms above their heads, holding up one end of a wooden beam thick enough to flatten a car. Both of them were red-faced and trembling.

"Help me," begged Kaley, looking at Emily. "I can't hold it."

Dante was gritting his teeth, but he managed to nod and utter a few words. "D-Do it. Save your friend."

But Emily was frozen. What could she do? How could she help them? Their arms were about to give way at any moment, and she was nowhere near strong enough to take up the slack. If they tried to drop it and run, it would crush them before they got their tired legs moving.

"Help me!" Kaley yelled. "Emily?"

Emily nodded. "I'm coming."

She started to walk, then trot, then run. Asking God for strength, she somehow made it into a sprint. She rushed towards Kaley, all of her focus engaged on gaining more and more speed.

Kaley nodded at Emily, her eyes desperately pleading. "Yes!"

Emily managed a final burst of speed and then threw herself forward.

She collided with Dante at full speed and sent him flying across the sand. She went with him, her momentum enough to send them both airborne. They crashed down six feet away and rolled three full rotations in a tangle of limbs and elbows. When they came to a stop, Emily was lying on top of Dante, staring into his eyes.

Kaley let out a short scream, immediately cut off.

Emily turned to look back at her friend.

Kaley was squashed beneath the wooden beam. Emily had barrelled into Dante quickly enough to knock him clear of danger, but Kaley had been too slow to get out. The thick length of wood now lay across her body diagonally, with only one of her legs and one arm still able to move. Half her head was pressed almost flat, and her left eye had popped out of its socket. Blood stained her lips.

Despite her pain, Kaley was still conscious, and still able to talk in breathless moans. "Em... Emily? Why?"

Emily crawled over the sand towards her dying friend. It took everything she had left. "The Kaley I knew would rather die than become a monster. I'm so sorry."

"You... You betrayed me."

"No, you made a mistake, and this was the only way to save you."

Kaley laughed, spitting blood. "Stupid..."

Emily let the tears fall down her face. "I wish none of this had ever happened. If I could change it..." She stared to sob. "Forgive me. Please. I love you."

"I... I..." Kaley sucked at air but could barely get any. "I... curse you. By the power... of... Klanek... I curse you to d-d-death."

"No."

Emily slumped sideways as her friend took her final breath and went still. Blood trickled from Kaley's mouth and her expression froze in place. The last of her friendship group was gone. All that remained was her.

Emily sobbed harder than she had ever sobbed in her life, not because her friend had just cursed her, but because she had refused to forgive her.

CHAPTER
TWENTY-ONE

"I NEED to work late tomorrow night," said John, loosening his tie and unbuttoning his white shirt enough to show his chest hair. "We have a stocktake."

Emily knew nothing about any stocktake, and why he had waited until closing time to bring it up, she didn't know. Maybe he just liked fucking with her. Maybe he was just trying to get her alone.

All the lights in the shop were off except for those at the front. She had just cashed up while John did whatever he did in the office. With her head down as she wrote figures down in the banking book, she told him, "I'm not working late tomorrow, John."

"I need you to."

"I don't care."

"This isn't a debate."

"You're right, it's not. I'm looking for another job, but in the meantime, I'm only working the hours I'm contracted to. If you don't like it, fire me."

"Emmie, what's got into you? I don't like this attitude."

She looked up at him from behind the desk. "I don't give a

fuck, John. Life is short, and I'm not spending all of it here. If this place is *your* life, then I suggest you get a new one."

John's mouth fell wide open, and the sight of him actually made her giggle. All the times he had innocently touched her – and other girls who had worked at the shop over the months – and all of the times he had screwed with her life just to feel like he had control over her… it all flashed through her mind like a movie reel.

She made up her mind. Putting her acting skills to use, she immediately changed tact, thrusting out her hip and smiling a lopsided grin. "Oh, calm down, John. If you're so desperate to get me alone, then you should just ask me out."

His mouth closed, fell open again, then closed again. He had to lick his lips before he could talk. "Wh-What are you talking about? I-I don't think of you like that, Emmie."

"Yeah, you do. I see the way you look at me. How often do you think about kissing me? How often do you think about putting your hands on my slender, young body?"

"Stop it. This is inappropriate."

You're the king of inappropriate, arsehole. "Come on," she purred. "Fess up. It's okay. I'm right here, aren't I? So do what you've been dying to do. Kiss me."

He was quivering like a terrified child, but she knew she had him. The way he was looking at her mouth was a dead giveaway. "Are you messing with me?"

She rolled her eyes. "Oh for Klanek's sake, let's get this over with." She reached out and grabbed his tie, yanking him forward over the desk. His lips tasted salty, and she was immediately repulsed, but she slipped him a little tongue.

He deserves that much at least.

When he put his hands around her hips, she shoved him away. The deed was done. No need for any more pretence. The kiss had left him out of breath, but now he was confused. "Wh-What are you doing?"

"I'm not usually a cruel person, John, but some guys just

have it coming, you know? I need to put a stop to all this madness and, unfortunately, you drew the short straw."

"What are you talking about? Emmie, where are you going? Let's lock up and go get a drink together, or maybe go to my place."

"No thanks. Oh, and I won't be here in the morning, but neither will you be. I think you're gonna have a really crappy night."

"I… I don't understand."

She went over to the exit, then turned to face him. "You're a perv, John. I don't know if you deserve to die or not, but I know that you deserve it more than I do. I'm sorry, I really am. Goodbye, John. And good luck."

She exited the shop, not even hearing the words he was muttering after her. In a few hours he would probably be dead, so she had to make sure she was nowhere near him. The last thing she needed was more questions from the police.

It had been six days since Kaley had cursed her, and she had almost died every day since. Klanek no longer wanted her in his service, so he tried all he could to claim her. Only Dante had kept her alive, employing charms and old blessings to ward off as much bad luck as he could. He had even got some of his fellow Syrians to pray for her, and they had helped him keep guard while she attempted to get through her days.

It had taken her six days to come to terms with passing the curse on to John. Fortunately, he had made it easy for her by constantly pawing at her and being an arsehole. He hadn't even cared when he'd found out her friends were dead. Dante had eventually convinced her that it was a simple equation – who deserved to live more? It took a while, but she had found enough self-love to admit that she was a far better person than John.

And now it was over. She had survived six days of a demon trying to kill her and dispatched her sex-pest of a boss. Life was looking up.

It started to look even better when she met Dante at the Rock.

"Is it done?" he asked her.

She nodded. "I'm free. I'm pretty much a murderer now, but I'm sure therapy will help."

He let out the longest breath, like a balloon deflating. "I've been so afraid of losing you, Ems. It's a miracle you made it so long. It must be Allah's doing."

"Or maybe Father Daniel's," she said. "I promised to attend Church every week if he prayed for me nightly for a whole month. He agreed."

"Then bless Father Daniel and Allah both."

She hopped onto the Rock and sat down beside him. The tide was out, the evening drawing in. Seagulls were commencing their nightly feast of cockles. For a while they sat in silence, their warm bodies touching.

Eventually, Dante spoke. "Have the police left you alone?"

"I think so. They have CCTV of Matt dying, so they know it was a freak accident. They also can't find a reason I would have had anything to do with Lily's death. They found Harry and Kaley's bodies under the pier together, so I think they're running with him being the killer. I told them Harry was aggressive and that he hit me. They had it on CCTV, too – as well as Kaley and Lily attacking him for it. It all points to Harry being a psycho. It doesn't make full sense, but they can't link me to murders I didn't commit, so they seem to be looking elsewhere finally. Good thing, too, because my mum is ready to have a heart attack."

"I look forward to meeting her."

She smiled at him. "Yeah, me too. Hey, any comeback with Steve?"

"No. My friends helped me dispose of him one night. We weighted him down and threw him in the canal. It was unkind, but we prayed for his soul. If he is ever found, there will be no clues for the police to find."

She sighed with relief. "Then we're good. No curses, no impending murder convictions. Just… life. Life without any of my friends, and the knowledge that they were all killed by a demon name Klanek. It's fine, right? Everything is going to be fine?"

"With any luck," he said.

Emily groaned and shoved him. He caught her arm and pulled her on top of him. They kissed for a while, and then rubbed noses together. She was falling in love, she knew it, and perhaps that was the only reason she hadn't walked herself into the sea and drowned. Not everything had been lost. A part of her was still alive. The part of her that yearned to be a part of Dante's life.

"I will always keep you safe," he told her.

"That sounds awesome, but I would rather not be in danger in the first place."

"Then I promise never to cause you tears."

She chuckled. "Seriously? Are all Syrian guys this into making promises? Look, just treat me with respect. That's all I want."

"Okay, okay. I promise to treat you with respect." He cleared his throat. "And always try to make you happy."

She rolled her eyes. "Fine. I'll accept that – and I promise the same. I'm sorry it wasn't always that way. I have a lot to learn, but I'm ready for it. No more coasting through life without responsibility. I'm going to be the best Emily I can be."

"I can't wait. You're already so perfect."

She kissed him on the mouth and then sat up. She stared out at the sea, enjoying the salty scent of the breeze. "No one's perfect, Dante. Life isn't about being perfect."

"Then what is it about?"

She shrugged. "Admitting that we know nothing, but trying our best anyway?"

"Yes, I think this is true."

"Anyway, I'm hungry. Want to eat?"

He nodded. "I have been dying to feed you my famous *yabrak*. You take some vine leaves and—"

She put a hand up. "Whoa, little steps, okay? I was thinking more about going down *Barney's Chippy*. You can get a kebab." Her eyes went wide and she gasped. "Was that racially insensitive of me?"

He looked at her. "What? No, I love kebab. Let's go."

They hopped off of the Rock, giggling, and then strolled down the promenade, holding hands. Emily was grieving for half a dozen people, but at least at that moment she was feeling all right. In fact, as she looked at the handsome man who she knew was also falling in love with her, she felt pretty lucky.

Don't miss out on your FREE Iain Rob Wright horror pack. Five terrifying books sent straight to your inbox.

No strings attached & signing up is a doddle.

Just Visit IainRobWright.com

ALSO BY IAIN ROB WRIGHT

Animal Kingdom
AZ of Horror
2389
Holes in the Ground (with J.A.Konrath)
Sam
ASBO
The Final Winter
The Housemates
Sea Sick, Ravage, Savage
The Picture Frame
Wings of Sorrow
Hell on Earth (6 books)
TAR
House Beneath the Bridge
The Peeling
Blood on the bar
Escape!
Dark Ride
12 Steps
The Room Upstairs
Soft Target, Hot Zone, End Play, Terminal
The Spread (6 books)
Witch
Zombie
Hell Train
Maniac Menagerie

Iain Rob Wright is one of the UK's most successful horror and suspense writers, with novels including the critically acclaimed, THE FINAL WINTER; the disturbing bestseller, ASBO; and the wicked screamfest, THE HOUSEMATES.

His work is currently being adapted for graphic novels, audio books, and foreign audiences. He is an active member of the Horror Writer Association and a massive animal lover.

www.iainrobwright.com
FEAR ON EVERY PAGE

For more information
www.iainrobwright.com
author@iainrobwright.com

Copyright © 2022 by Iain Rob Wright

Cover Photographs © Shutterstock

Artwork by Carl Graves at Extended Imagery

Editing by Richard Sheehan

All rights reserved.

No part of this book may be reproduced in any form or by any electronic or mechanical means, including information storage and retrieval systems, without written permission from the author, except for the use of brief quotations in a book review.

❦ Created with Vellum

Printed in Great Britain
by Amazon